KING DRAGON

Andrew J. Offutt

SF
ace books
A Division of Charter Communications Inc.
A GROSSET & DUNLAP COMPANY
51 Madison Avenue
New York, New York 10010

KING DRAGON

An ACE Book

First Ace printing: October 1980

2 4 6 8 0 9 7 5 3 1
Manufactured in the United States of America

This novel
is dedicated to
Jodie Offutt
because I love her

with special thanks to
James Patrick Baen
who instigated it;
Ruth Kaplan and Jefferson Offutt
Technical Advisors *extraordinaires;*
and
Jerry Pournelle and Carl Sagan,
whose articles suggested it;

and
Burroughs, Doyle, Haggard, Howard, Wells,
and all the others who wrote
Lost World novels
back when they were patently impossible
and never knew that science and technology
would make them feasible and . . . possible?

ACCORDING TO PLAN, THE TORUS-SHIP THAT BROUGHT US HERE IS NOW THE STATION ORBITING THE PLANET: OUR HOME WHILE WE MAKE THE PLANET LIVABLE. LIKE EARTH, IT IS THIRD FROM ITS SUN (THOUGH ORBITING IT A BIT CLOSER). UNLIKE EARTH, IT IS AN ENEMY TO HUMANKIND. SEE-OH-TWO COMPOSES 97.373 PERCENT OF THE ATMOSPHERE, WHICH IS SO THICK THAT THE PLANETARY SURFACE IS INVISIBLE. PROBE REPORTS PRESSURE OF 80 EARTH-ATM. AND TEMPERATURE IN EXCESS OF THREE HUNDRED SEES.

Staring at the printout of the recorded message across centuries and lightyears, Allayth shook his head. "Never occurred to me that carbon dioxide prints out as words—'see-oh-two'—and that C for Centigrade comes out the same: 'sees'."

Flaerti looked mildly indulgent and let the younger man see that it required some strain. "It has been that way for over a thousand years, Candidate."

Flustered, Allayth tried to cover and of course said too much. "I never saw it in print before, I mean. Not spelled out. As words, I mean, rather than . . ." He stopped himself. Laxshmy had told him that he tended to babble when he was excited or embarrassed, and he didn't really need to be told. Being aware of the problem and getting a

1

grip on the handle to turn it off, he had discovered, were two different things.

Flaerti said absolutely nothing and the silence was so thick, so audible to Allayth that he had to clench his jaw to prevent further babbling. It wasn't a crime, after all, and no one suspected him of being anything approaching stupid. But did Senior Scholar Flaerti think of him as an ass? Allayth could never be sure, which made him just that much less comfortable with the man. Already his heartbeat was up. And now this message—he punched up the rest of that message sent out so long ago, and let it cover for him.

FROM ORBIT, IN A FEW MINUTES WE WILL BEGIN POURING ON THE A-NOSTOCACEA-3 *COLI*. ALL ABOARD *HAJAR L'ILLAH* ARE DEDICATED, AND PREPARED. THIS MUST BE OUR HOME FOR MANY YEARS. WE WILL SURVIVE UP HERE, AS WE HAVE ON OUR JOURNEY HERE, WHILE OUR BLUE-GREEN ALGAE WORK THEIR WAY DOWN TO THE PLANET. EATING UP SEE-OH-TWO AND SPITTING OUT OH-TWO, AS THE CAPTAIN PUTS IT. IT TOOK A HUNDRED YEARS FOR THE PREVIOUS STRAIN OF THIS SAME B-G ALGAE TO LIBERATE WATER VAPOR AND PRECIPITATE THE BIG RAIN ON VENUS. AN IMPROVED STRAIN CUT THAT TIME TO 77 YEARS ON CARMEIS, TO CREATE ITS NITROGEN-OXYGEN ATMOSPHERE AND WASH AWAY UNDESIRABLE . . . JUNK. HERE WE EXPECT TO CREATE A WATER TABLE IN FOUR DECADES OR LESS. NO MORE THAN FOUR. I SHALL SEE IT! ALLAH ISELMAK! BAH'RAM ISELMAK!

" 'Bah'ram be praised,' eh?" Flaerti murmured, and a sneer rode his voice like a blight on a leaf. "I had forgotten that we created Venus—I

mean, made it livable. Earth-like, I mean. And
Carmeis is so—Sorry. I *must* be excited! This message was sent . . . how long ago, Senior?"

Natharam ibben Flaerti seemed to squint because of the ancient eyeglass he affected. A one-
eye, it was called: almonocol. (Allayth, who knew
ancient Arabic as well as Terrali, was aware that
the word was a frightful bastardization. Though
he knew no Greek at all, he accepted that the word
had been sired by two Greek ones, and then born
of an Inglis mother to enter Arabic long ago as
al-monoc'l, eventually to become "almonocol" in
Terrali. Jimajin Allayth had not concentrated on
language. Not even this one. Language interested
him and was an aid to his studies and researches.
One could clutter one's head with only so much
arennai—which he did know came from the old
abbreviation "RNA." What that stood for was

hardly worth remembering. It was not always the most pleasant, remembering everything one heard or read.)

Staring at nothing in particular, Flaerti seemed to squint a bit behind the plasilica device he affected over one eye—which was of course perfectly sighted. Imperfect sight, like imperfect teeth and the hypertension sub-gene, was buried with the past. It was good that at ninety-six years of age Flaerti was still so youthful as to Play Past. Everyone did. Allayth wore boots of leather-imitating polymer equhyde, with real side-zippers, and amused himself with a black-and-white modifier for his homescreen. He was genuinely good with bow and arrows, and now and again joined others in working out with stave and shield. Everyone Played Past, one way or another. The Past was better. Everyone said so.

"This message," Senior Scholar Natharam ibben Flaerti said to an area somewhere east of him he surely considered a mere boy of twenty-four, "was sent just under a thousand years ago. Tight," he said, and his pause separated the word into its components, "beam."

"A thou . . . sand years . . . sss ago-ohh," Allayth whispered with the reverence of a scholar, if not quite Scholar. And then it hit him. "Why, there's a colony there! A culture! People! They've been there . . . hundreds of years!"

"If they survived, yes."

"And we have never heard anything before, never found them . . ."

Flaerti gave him an excellent imitation of a man about to smile. "There is more."

There was.

It told Allayth that once Jauhar al-Ajr was terra-formed in what was called the Cytherean manner or saganation, it would become the longtime dream of someone called al-Bah'ram: a controlled, observed experiment in evolution. Aboard the ship of The Bah'ram's followers were various embryos modified by recombinant DNA and bio- or genetic-engineering; genengineering. Feline embryos. Canine and ursine embryos. Saurian: lizard eggs in suspended incudevelopment. And . . .

"Humans!"

"Humans," Flaerti nodded, without twitching at the outburst he might well have expected. "There may or may not be *people* on Jauhar al-Ajr, Candidate Allayth. The only people may be in orbit many kilometers above the planet, in a very strange society indeed. A society alien to us. For they will be people who have never set foot on the ground, or breathed air in the open—and neither have their predecessors for nine hundred years."

Allayth was dizzied. What a concept—O God and Stars, the compass of this! An entire culture existed out there. Planned, controlled. Not one single person was a descendant of ordinary genes. And all within the enclosed "world" of their making: an orbiting station that had doubled as the spaceship that took them there. Over hundreds of years this ship-society had existed there, a planet-less culture. Plenty of time for such a society to grow and develop, he mused. And surely to become hidebound, inbred of citizen and custom. (Or perhaps they didn't breed, but cloned instead, again and again. His brain tried to pounce on that and Allayth yanked it away like a man whose foot has tangled in a vine.) Plenty of time to evolve, to adapt and grow tighter both at once, to produce its own customs and mores, its own laws and necessary rules; codes and fashions. (Perhaps they used a solar parasol or two to maintain such a warmth that no one bothered with clothing at all. That seemed sensible and desirable to him, without his taking time to give it any real thought or consideration.) *And no foot has ever touched ground*, his fibrillating mind babbled. Not one of the descendants of that carefully chosen crew—what crew had not been?—had ever walked in the open, looked up at the sky; felt the warmth of a naked sun or the caress of a breeze, felt or even heard rain. And all the while, down on the planet they had revised and so peculiarly seeded so long ago—what? Allayth swallowed. He felt weak in the legs and head. Even his heartbeat was up and his armpits prickled.

Just to read a diary or treatise on such a culture would be new, wonderful! To visit, to see it . . . I'd give a hand.

With considerable effort, he set himself at entropy and spoke only when he knew he had come down. A bit.

"This . . . Bah'ram?"

"I have sought and found, and I congratulate you on thinking of it, Jim. He was the expedition's leader and absolute commander. A fabulously, ridiculously wealthy fanatic who persuaded the Saudistani government to supply the ship—while he financed everything else, personally! He can be said to have fled Earth, leading an expedition whose every member was pure-blooded Arabic."

"There is . . . there never was any such, such

thing. No such— 'Arabic' was a language and 'al-Islam' an area of the world named after the religion. 'Arab' was never a race."

"The Candidate becomes a pedant," Flaerti said mildly, though without smiling. "Say non-Jewish Semitics from the old middle eastern land of Saudistan, then. This Bah'ram was also an unusually brillaint biochemist—for his time—and took with him no less than a two B.M.D.'s of considerable brilliance."

Two of the ancient Bioengineers! Allayth reconsidered and decided he would give the whole arm, not just the hand, to visit the Bah'ram's station and the planet he had chosen to name "Jewel of Heaven": Jauhar al-Ajr. Either hand, taker's choice; Allayth was after all ambidextrous. A clever bit of genengineered self-indulgence on his parents' part, that.

"What . . . what do we, what will we I mean Earth do about . . . we can't just ignore . . ."

"My impression is frequently that your brain and body want to act together, Candidate, and when your body cannot, your mouth fails to cooperate with your brain."

Allayth concentrated on looking chastised. True. All he wanted to be doing was jumping up and down.

"Observation of a culture without changing the culture is still impossible, isn't it, Candidate?"

"Yes," Allayth said miserably, and then he frowned. Was he being teased?

"No, Jim, we cannot and will not ignore. You have completed your course of study, I know, and are among the best of Candidates."

Among the best! Allayth thought with a surge of

threatened pride, but then he remembered Laxshmy. Yuh, she was the best, top graduate and
high Candidate, and unable to forget it for longer
than an hour or two—only when they were in bed.
She was unable to cease chafing, or even to be
natural and happy with him despite their efforts
and the seeming destined naturalness of their
antemarriage. Amid sprawling pawing panting
animalistic wonders of what they called Aristote-
lean Love—black and white, though that referred
only to the color of their hair and "love" was
hardly the word—they had anguished, together
and separately. They had racked brains and com-
puters in search of that increasingly elusive
Original Contribution necessary to the attaining
of a Scholar's rank. Meanwhile Laxshmy periodi-
cally lapsed into her superiority syndrome. And
the bitterness, naturally, though it was true she
coped with it better than he did. He was sure she
kept a few ideas and thoughts back, too. Should
she hit upon a subject, a project, it would be hers,
not theirs. Unless they agreed to co-work and
obtained permission to do, she would go off into it
and that would be that for Jimajin Allayth—and
for Jim and Laxy Rainio.

So much for his superiority, and for his security. And he, too, had slid off into this too fre-
quent gulley of thoughts and doubts, while Senior
Scholar Flaerti was speaking to him—of him!

"At sixteen you had the learning to have made
you what was called a 'Doctor of Philosophy' back
in the Transition Era. In a way it was harder then;
they had to go to school physically, and be taught;
to memorize data. Now we know that attaining
Scholar's rank, their PhD, was easy back when

humankind was just prying into space and toying fearfully with recom-deenai and potential monsters whose name ended in *coli*, and had never made that first solar umbrella."

Oh thanks, Allayth thought, and he was restless and felt the miseries coming on. *I really need all this*—

"I know with what anguish you have been waiting for years for a subject to be found approvable for your Scholar Contribution and Thesis. I know you have tried three times—formally, and doubtless discarded other potential subjects without ever presenting them for consideration by the Bureau of Savants."

Flaerti was talking calmly, dully, and giving pain. Yet Jim Allayth stared and couldn't quite breathe while he waited. Was he—could he be leading up to—

Yes! "You have found it, Jim. Your Subject has come in by tight-but-deflected-beam from light-years away. You are going out to Jauhar, Jim—or to a station orbiting the sun Jibrail III—unless you object. It could well make you the youngest Senior Scholar in decades."

Even trembling with excitement, afraid to believe and daring not try to say anything, his brain a canoe churning in a maelstrom, Jim Allayth had the thought: *For a hundred and six years, if I can get out there and back and publish within the next four years!*

2

The jumpship brought itself closer to the Jibrail system of nine planets. On board, Jim Allayth was excited and heartened by this mission that was his great chance. At the same time, he brooded. Once he had recovered from the marvelous shock of Flaerti's announcement, Allayth had thought to ask whether Laxshmy Rainio would—could—accompany him. It was then that he had received the day's second big surprise, and again he gained the news from Natharam Flaerti. Laxshmy had filed for termination of their trial relationship, only the day before. "Under the circumstances," Flaerti explained, "it hardly seemed wise to close you two up together in a jumpship! Too, it was easy, Jim, to decide that both our top Scholar Candidates should not be off-Earth together. There are potential hazards in this project, you know."

Next came the ugliest scene ever, between Rainio and Allayth. She blew up about his going alone. She could not or would not believe that they would most likely have been sent out together had she not filed to terminate their ante-marriage. Eventually, during shouting recriminations, accusations, and re-recriminations, she had let slip that she had a potentially excellent subject for her Scholar Project. . . . End argument, end relationship.

Allayth thought about that now, far and far from Earth and Laxshmy and the quarters they had shared. But not far enough from the memories. That distance would not be measured in kilometers or light years. Elated and deflated, sad and glad, glad and sad: Jimajin Allayth, Candidate for Scholardom. Too many memories, and so young. The past was better . . .

Next had come the battle with Council. Savants versus bureaucrats. The latter wanted to send an Official Delegate who was a career diplomat; a government exosociologist team; an exopsychologist; a "security observer" from CSP; a militarist . . . all of whom would necessitate a larger ship and more preparations and would be senior to Allayth, who after all had neither diplomatic nor government nor field experience.

For once, Savantry won—though by now Allayth was not so sure. More likely economics had won. At least the government exosociologist bore no resemblance to Laxshmy. As a matter of fact she was considerably less pretty and less rangy though hardly luxuriously constructed, and both her hair and eyes were dark. Now, though, within Jibrail's galaxy, he strongly suspected that exosoc. Cicada Lurie was also the Council Security Protection "observer." As for the ambassador: Gadnason had proved an absolute pain. In his manner, in his superiority, and in his determination to possess Cicada Lurie. (And once, Jim thought without being certain, Gadnason had wanted Jimajin Allayth?)

Both Allayth and Lurie pretended concern and remorse-sympathy when the poor intelligent idiot accomplished the near-impossible: his own demise.

There was nothing heroic about it, or even properly tragic, that death in outer space. Senior Diplomat Hwawng Gadnason failed in one vital procedure—and drowned in less than a tenth of a liter of carbonated drink. Raspberry.

He was hideous. Closing his eyes was not easy and did not help. They discussed, rather wistfully, burying him in space. They did not. They refrigerated him. And the good ship *Cygnet* plunged on, tiny but not quite cramped, while Allayth attained one of the departed diplomat's goals, without half trying. After the death he and Cicada ("Sick-ada," Gadnason had called her, once printing it out so there could be no mistake about the division of the syllables) both needed life, solace, comfort. Each provided it for the other, and after that there was no reason to stop.

Then they came into normal space, and that big bright ball was Jibrail, and with only a little help *Cygnet* did what it was supposed to do: it conveyed them in toward the smallish sun's third planet, 155 million kilometers out. The two inner ones must have been crisps; orbiting cinders. Jim and Cicada saw the little outermost satellite, which would be a mere point of light as seen from Jauhar.

"Retrograde," she said, merely commenting.

"Yuh. There's another."

Computer said it was moving in the way they thought of as normal. And kept taking them in, without seeking orbit. They found a third satel-

lite. Its size was about a third that of the second and it was perhaps half its distance from Jauhar. To call its orbit "rapid" was to understate.

"One wonders," she said. She talked that way, and she had one doubly-pierced ear, too, and was fond of spraYon pants. "Is it romantic, a moon that comes up more than once in a night?"

He smiled. "Oftener than that: every five-and-a-quarter hours! It's a long night down there. Over fifty of our hours. What I wonder about is tides. And stomachs."

"Stomachs?"

"Say bio-clocks," he said. "I'm just thinking about how often one gets hungry—and sleepy!—on a planet with a day that's several days long. Earth-days, I mean. We might—"

"*There it is!*"

ARTIFICIAL SATELLITE ONSCREEN.

There it was. *It* was the object of their quest and their mission. Not the planet called Jauhar, but its metal satellite, with the fantastic and fabulous thousand-year-old extraplanetary culture that so excited both Allayth and Lurie. Cygnet, which demonstrably needed no pilot (or "astrogator" as some still pretentiously persisted in saying) moved in. They would fall in behind The Bah'ram's "world" of metal in a matching orbit—but slightly farther out from the planet. And they would overtake. Allayth set the automatic frequency scanner; Lurie reached too late for the autocontinuous tightcaster and watched it cut in by itself.

Both of them had expressed the feeling that the damned ship would have been perfectly happy without their cluttering presence aboard. Happier. Now she commented on Allayth's speed of action, too.

"You do tend to act faster than I can think, you know that?"

"Who thinks?" His gaze was on readouts and telltales.

She chuckled dutifully. "What do you think we're going to find?" she said, almost whispering while she stared at busy dials and telits. Her left earring, a slim loop of hollow and almost weightless alloy indistinguishable from silver, swung and glittered. The hoop's diameter was eight centimeters and she liked it better than he did.

He watched the steady blipping of the proximity telit, each blip showing a lower number. "A stratified society," he said, staring at the gauge because he could not look away. "Rites, rigid customs and so on."

"Like Scholars, Savants, and the necessity for Original Contribution as rite of passage?"

He forgot to smile. "Worse, Rigidity, surely. Iron discipline. Surely there would have to be, in this sort of tight little enclosed . . . world. Tightly controlled births, too."

Closer, closer.

"I still think there are no births. Sex for recreation, cloning for regeneration-continuity."

"That's sensible," he said. Staring was necessary and talking was preferable to tension-heightening silence. "We could probably postulate a hundred ideas, both broad and specific and a lot of them with high probability, and still miss on ninety-seven. Clothing makes sense. Even loose clothing. Or just decoration, in what can't be a very pretty environment. And nudity makes just as much sense."

"Nudity never makes sense, Jim. Not societal nudity, I mean."

He didn't agree and didn't care to argue. Both of them were talking to themselves while staring at the instrument readings. "Do you believe in clothing-as-coverup or clothing-as-decoration?"

"Yes."

Closer, closer.

"Was the first loincloth a loose flap to cover the genitals from the eyes of others—or to draw attention, create a bit of mystery by decorating? Or was it a sling, to hold these so-vulnerable ornaments hung on us males for our sins?"

She smiled, looking genuinely merry. "And for your sinning! Try running or jumping with bare breasts of any size. Or even harnessed big ones. We females got stuck with those for our sins, I guess. In really warm climates, though, people didn't invent brassieres, or briefs, or even breechclouts, often. They did invent some sort of cover for women to wear several days each month, and in some societies that was mandatory. Which brings us back to 'sin'!"

"Or complete withdrawal from society," he said. "Also mandatory among some peoples."

"Which brings us back to 'sin'!"

"You've got sinning on the mind, 'Skada. And some peoples of some hot climates did too wear loin covers of this or that sort, males or females or both. And paint, which must have been hot."

"White would tend to reflect sun, Jimajin, rather than absorb—"

He stared at the blip-blipping proximity telit, as if hypnotized by the countdown movement it showed. Closer, closer. "Stupid of them to wear blue paint, then, not to mention red and black."

They raced along behind the spaceborne wheel that was The Bah'ram's station; Station Jauhar. *Cygnet* was scanning, sensing, listening, broadcasting, probing. A small oblong screen flashed to life. Another. An oval, grass-green. They began learning about Station Jauhar. Item by item, they learned.

Radiation count: minuscule.

Torque: nonexistent. Frowning, Allayth punched a request for more details. He got them, succinctly: no spin was detectable of or on Station.

"They're living without gravity?" Cicada said, wondering aloud.

Solar umbrella: holed, semi-collapsed, *not* turned sunward.

NO TRACE OF HEAT. NONE. RPT ZERO

Allayth punched and tapped. "Solar? Ultraviolet? Rads? No heat is impossible."

(UV: *High!* [Apparent] mechanical heat, body heat: ZERO)

NO EMISSIONS

(Allayth and Lurie did not look at each other. Cygnet moved nearer, nearer. If they had a window, they could see the great wheel. If they had a window.)

SOLAR SHIELDS: FUNCTION OR NONFUNCTION UNCERTAIN

(PROBABILITY: HOLED ERGO NONFUNCTIONING)

RAD COUNT: 0.2.2ENR

APPARENT MECHANICAL HEAT/BODY HEAT: ZERO RPT ZERO

TECHNO-EMISSIONS: ZERO

"No!"

No trace of flotsam, exhaust . . . well, Allayth

mused, happy to refute something, who'd expect such, anyhow? In such a situation as these people were in, everything would be recycled, one way or another; everything.

UV: HIGH. NO TRACE OF GENERATED/RADIATED HEAT. NONE.

"No! Rpt!"

REPEAT: GEN/RAD HEAT: ZERO

"Keep looking!" (No reply. Reply was as unnecessary as the admonition. All probesystemry, all seeksystemry, all scanning systems were ON and would remain ON.)

ZERO HEAT. NO TRACE OF RADIANT HEAT.

NO EMISSIONS.

[APPARENT] ACTIVITY: ZERO RPT ZERO

"What? Confirm!"

CONFIRMED. EMISSIONS: ZERO

Humans created emissions. No signs of technology, energy-use yielding emissions: no humans.

"Interface with subject's scanners/sensors."

ATTEMPT ONGOING

"A thousand years," Cicada Lurie murmured. "Why not? Maybe . . . maybe they all went on-planet. Maybe they had to? Trouble up here. A revolt, maybe. A thousand years! Their lives and mental and physical well-being merely observing controlled evolution."

"Interface/link with subject's computer!"

ATTEMPT ONGOING

EMISSIONS ZERO

PRESSURE—

ATTEMPTING TO MEASURE PRES

ATTEMPTING TO FIND RECORDABLE PRESSURE

Allayth did not speak No! No. They are there.

They must be there. I want them to be there. They are there. His sides tickled from trickling sweat and his heart was pounding—he discovered that he had been holding his breath and began controlled breathing—and he had gone all quivery and hot, hot. More reports came rushing as they drew closer and closer, inrushing but unfinished as more important new data superseded; data tumbling over data, readouts vanishing uncompleted to be replaced by others:

RADCOUNT 0.2.197ENR

NO CONTACT

RADCOUNT INSUFFICIENT TO INDICATE HABI

PRESSURE ZERO RPT ZERO

UNABLE TO DETECT VITAL SI

ATMOSPHERIC PRESSURE ZERO RPT ZERO

3

Sai, who told stories and called himself poet and was called pretentious by some for his choice of words and phrasings, waited with her. They sat amid the aroma of extravagant fungi that mingled with the pungent scent of the conifers surrounding Kwait. And the odor of the people themselves, of Kwait.

"All Kwait has held its breath throughout all the hours since the last sleep, awaiting judgment of you," he said, speaking low. He was staring at the ground. He had been poking at it with a long, curved sabretooth. A gift, of course. Sai killed nothing. "Doesn't that make you feel important?"

"No," she said in automatic response. She gazed at him, considering what he had said, until she had to blink in what was almost a voluntary action. She caught his meaning. That was part of her multiform problem, that she caught his meaning. (Feel important? She was incapable.) Sai had not spoken literally. Certainly every member of the community had not held its breath all these hours, else all would be dead. Yet all the people of Kwait, and thus in a way his "all Kwait," shared the suspense, the apprehension. Even anticipation in some cases, she was sure. At such times

people held their breaths, as she had just held her
sad-eyed gaze until her eyes were so dry they
started to hurt. And so all quiet-voiced Sai de-
vised and made his statement, in the way of a
tale-teller. Many would not have understood, at
least not at once. Kwait did not exist or speak or
think in the abstract. All were sure that God and
his Messenger frowned on such. Abstractions and
metaphors birthed no children and fed none. Still,
such a way of giving talk was Approved when it
came from a tale-teller, provided that he did not
deviate over far from God's Own Language.

God lived. None saw him, but all saw his Messenger. The world was blessed with a living God.
And his Messenger. They saw him fly over from
time to time: King Dragon.

The language was like unto Allah—no, it was
more changeless and immutable even than God.
For he had been known to change his mind, and
his Messenger had worn other forms. So legend
said.

She did not call Sai pretentious or dangerous in
his language, or think him so. She liked him. She
was grateful to him. She liked him a lot, and could
like him more, for all his pronounced and even
cultivated eccentricities. At present, for instance,
he had not scraped his face all this day of two
sleeps and three sunwakes, and in addition he
unaccountably wore a perfectly ordinary stone on
a thong about his neck. It was not decorative. She
would not ask why he wore it, and probably no
one else would. It was an eccentricity. Oh Sai
would have a reason, but it might or might not
make sense to anyone else. He was the tale-teller.
In him, strangeness was accepted.

He was lean, and hardly the mightiest of fight-ers, Sai son of Sayyar; Sai Tale-teller. Nor was his lean, lean face among the five best-favored of the young males of Kwait. He was a good stalker—though no more than good—yet hardly competent at doing something about the game he stalked or happened upon. Sai Tale-teller, who walked alone. (*O God, Allahuma, he walks alone because it is his wish and his way! Why must I? I want only to be a woman, a woman like other women. Why am I waiting judgment or two choices? Either only guarantees more misery for me!*)

Once Sai had picked and eaten the wrong mushroom and was sick for days and hardly him-self in the mind. All thought he would die, in that psychotropic delirium. He had not died. He had even maintained—and still did, if the matter were brought up—that he had eaten the jannfruit *delib-erately*. Delirium, Sai said, was good for a tale-teller. Doubtless God frowned at that, but what was one to do; he was the Tale-teller! The jinni-inhabited mushroom had poisoned him and afflicted him with delirium dreams, but no jinni had come for him. Sai lived. He was liked as tale-tellers are liked; or tolerated, with allowances made. Still, many made jest of his attempts at fishing, and his eccentricities. And no one would eat mushrooms plucked by Sai Tale-teller.

She gazed at him from under her lashes, while they waited for the time of judgment. He had little skill with weapons or at wrestling, and was not interested in either. (The Tale-teller of Kwait sup-pressed and controlled his aggressions by con-taining them, turning them in on himself and letting them seethe and ferment. They bubbled within him to spur new stories that were as often soft tales of people as they were accounts of mighty deeds.)

Because of this and his leanness and his eccentricities that others could not bear because they did not share them or the reasons, younger boys had picked fights with him again and again. Hunters had scars because they were hunters; Sai had a scar because he was different.

No one had guessed that it had anything to do with Sai, that coming of the Messenger of God one day, on wings big as bear-hides. (Well, nearly.) That terrible dragonish rukh or pterosaur landed, of course, on Skyreach Butte above Kwait. The *Omda*, Leader, had climbed up the face of the bluff. All grey and tan and shadow. He went to speak with King Dragon, Messenger of Allah, and he wore only his softsoles and unspotted crotcher. He bore no weapons. All in Kwait waited, watching the strange sheer hill of rock. It was bereft of all vegetation save scrubby evergreens that jutted at odd angles in shapes of elongated triangles. The people of Kwait had waited. Eventually they had seen the Messenger leap from the precipice to spread vast leathery wings equipped with claws. They saw him open and flap those wings like hide. Watched him catch and steady himself in air and flap, flap, to soar and flap away over the forest. Allah's own Messenger! *Malik-rukh!*

The Leader had come down from the mount, then, and some swore that until then none of the hairs on his chest had been grey. It was no tiny endeavor or feat, looking into the bright golden eyes of the Messenger of the Living God. He was an awesome sight and presence, and a fearsome one even to the leader of Kwait; *Omda al-Kwait*.

He had not addressed them then, though they had all been waiting anxiously. Instead he paced silently among his people, through them, unarmed and less gauded then they, to his home. When he emerged, he wore the Lion. Thus all knew that he spoke for the Living God. Layth al'illah spoke:

"The Peace of God and his Bah'ram—be he blessed and live eternal—be with you," he said, as they knew he would, and he waited, while their "And with you, O Omda," was dutifully droned.

Soon, she thought while she waited now with Sai, *soon She will emerge wearing the Lion. Then I shall know my fate; more lonely alone-ness, or banishment, or mate of horror!*

That day years ago, though, it had been the Leader who wore the Lion to tell them of the Messenger's words. He told them that once again they had failed in the eternal attempt at achieving

perfection; and that the Cooling must come again
upon them. A harbinger it was, a reminder: a mere
taste of the Cold Hell. They sighed and groaned,
but he had not done talking. He told them then
that Sai was thereafter apprenticed to Khareem
the Teller of Tales, and would be Tale-teller after
him and so was under the omda's protection at
peril of a transgressor's being taken by the Messenger of God. All were astounded. King Dragon
had come and spoken of Sai—skinny Sai! Thus
was he importanced beyond any other save the
omda and Her, the Speaker of Judgments.

Sai was ennobled while the people of Kwait
were more than intimidated.

After that Sai was no longer picked on.
Khareem died that very year too, during the Cooling when people sometimes wore skins over more
than their loins and breasts, and much more
bright gaudery to coax the Warming to return.

(Kwait had never achieved perfection. Not
once. The Cooling came upon them every year, at
the time when the configuration of stars called
The Spearman lost his spearpoint. It remained
and eased and went away after about the same
length of time on each occasion, when The
Spearman's point could dimly be seen returning
to tip his skyborne weapon. Then they gathered
cones and needles for the Great Cleaning and Re-
newal, and made new spearpoints for the First
Hunt.)

So did Sai Sayyar's son became the Tale-teller
of Kwait, though he had lived a sum of only nineteen years of 366 sleeps—seventy-three days. She
was his age plus eighteen sleeps, and had been
taller, then. (She was not now. Sai had got his

growth late, as boys sometimes did, during his twentieth year. She had grown no taller, but had unthickened here and there and grown more rounded while indenting, here and there, in a way that accentuated the new roundness of womanhood.) Her name was Joharah, though the final glottal was always swallowed. Hence she was called Johara.

Johara. Not moody, back then. She had cared and thought little of Sai then, though she did tend to be different from other maidens: she thought of more than muscle and handsome faces; prowess and small tight bottoms. It was the year of her mating with Yaseer, whom she did not love but neither hated. A good mating. A handsome, well-favored couple. She would bear well, Johara would. Everyone said so.

They were wrong, wrong!

She had wept both for Yaseer and for herself, when on the third day of their marriage he went on the hunt and became the prey. A mother threehorn, naturally suspicious and protective of her hideous calf, charged. Yaseer, turning to run, fell. By the time she finished trampling there was nothing of him worth bringing in. There was not even vengeance. For the Code of Bah'ram forbade the slaying of any placental or pouched mother before her young had lived a year. Except in defense of one's life, of course. Vengeance was hardly self defense.

Bride and widow, in three days. She had lain with her husband thirteen times in those 484 hours.

In all too short a time the widow Joharah was made to endure much of blade-sharp tongues, and she had hardly been happy. She abode. The widow Joharah mourned herself and was prey to every misery of depression and self-doubt unto despair. At times it seemed to her that to be dead would be no terrible thing. During that dark time she appreciated Sai, for he became friend to her. (Scandalizing all in Kwait by piercing one ear and hanging therefrom a glittering ring.) (Joharah was not scandalized.) Assuredly he was no more than friend to her. So, after a time, did Raafar Saurslayer befriend her, and soon after that he and her father arranged the betrothal.

Raafar Saurslayer was nice to look upon, and uncommonly mighty. He was nearly a giant. Muscles bulged on him like the gnarly branches of soaring trees and his legs were great roots. A mighty, mighty hunter, beloved of the Leader. He approached her father and Sai Tale-teller did not, nor was Joharah unhappy at that. Oh, she felt no *love* for Raafar. He was too sure, too arrogant—with cause, of course. But no woman of Kwait could have said with truth that she would not be happy to wed him.

She who had previously wed Raafar Saurslayer had been much envied and of course disliked and deferred to all at once. She had died. A failed childbirth, during the Cooling. Nor had the child—a daughter—survived. Some said she had died because God deemed a daughter unworthy of the mighty hunter Raaf Saurslayer. Of course he had fulfilled the time of mourning, and then waited to be sure that Joharah was not with the child of Yaseer.

A year after the death of his first wife, Joharah was betrothed to the giant and people began to treat her differently, again. She felt good again, and of worth; a woman and a part of Kwait. Mighty Raafar even promised a Kingsaur as bride-gift. (Even then she wondered: But where was one to wear one of those horrendous teeth long as a hand?—well, long as a middle finger, anyhow.)

4

The airlock closed. Two helmeted heads glanced at each other. Regardless of rules or drill, the larger one tugged loose a gauntlet. The inner port opened. Two suited bipeds entered the ship. The airlock closed. Allayth already had his helmet undogged, despite the quiver of his hand.

"Murdered!" He was almost shouting.

Her gauntlet dropped. Her helmet came off to clunk and rattle on the decking. She nodded and he saw that her hair was stringy with sweat. It need never be hot in a spacesuit; it was not. Both thermostats and both in-suit aircons were functional. And he too was sweating.

"No meteor shower did that, and surely no Mysterious Aliens From Outer Outer Space! They were murdered!"

She nodded. "Five holes," she said dully. "Five compartments, each holed. Sixth compartment gone, completely gone. Could it have been a sealed craft for maneuvering in atmosphere?"

"Or for escape. It must have been the command compartment. Even the parasol destroyed! Someone murdered Station Jauhar and everyone on it. In it. Everyone! No one went down on-planet, unless it was the murderer—the captain!"

"Or—some kind of rebel leader or squad," she pointed out thoughtfully.

"Someone! Hundreds of years ago! Centuries. Murdered! A nice stable orbit, even a few functioning systems. An orbiting coffin . . ."

"Mausoleum."

"Yes. Mausoleum. Memorial-in-orbit. Damn!" He was shaking and he whirled to swing at a bulkhead—and thought to pull the punch, even in the big gauntlet. He untoggled it, let it drop. Impatient, shaking, stricken, he had pulled the other one off in the airlock to be able to get at his helmet. "Yes," he whispered. "A mausoleum. Dust and splotches on the walls, all those splotches— God!"

5

Year 37: Al-Bah'ram spoke today of the progress on the planet below. His voice is so
strong, so commanding. So it was in my
father's time! What a man, our Leader!
—journal of Ah'met ibn Talal, Station Jauhar

In his pride, Raafar went forth in search of that
huge flesh-eating lizard that walked on two legs
and preyed on its own saurian kind—and anything else of flesh. It was a more than formidable
quarry. Years ago Joharah had watched, shuddering uncontrollably, while a Kingsaur attacked one
of those shield-necked nosehorns called bumblecow. The very ground trembled, and the tree in
which she squatted, clinging, half a kilometer
away. The tail of the Kingsaur was long as the
bumblecow's body—four meters and more. With
that long curving horn on its snout the lower-
slung beast had raked and thrust. Kingsaur, towering above, bit and snapped while it danced
ponderously with an eerie lightness of foot. Fifty
tons of carnivorous killer which, bleeding,
slightly staggering, slew and made its meal off the
other armored saurian. Joharah had not come
down from her spidertree until the victor had

stamped off and even the sound of its crashing feet was dimmed by distance and intervening forest.

It was not her place to plead with Kwait's mightiest hunter to eschew such a quest. Even before the Warming had given away to the time of heat that would peak in Ramadan, Raaf and his pride went forth. He bore spear and shield and the enormous stone ax only he could swing to effect, with one arm that was bigger than Joharah's thigh. He must go; he had promised. The mating would wait; he had promised. A promise was a promise was a vow was an oath before Allah and al-Bah'ram and Malik-rukh. Rule and rite dominated content and rationality among his people, and such considerations were more pronounced in Raafar son of Alal than in any other.

Joharah, bride-was, and bride-to-be, waited.

And waited. The time of great heat that was Ramadan dragged by and her fast was more rigorous than anyone's. The new attention that was hers began to change in tone. And Ramadan passed, with its heat and the fasting. Raafar had not returned.

Once again the Cooling came: Zamhar'. The fear it brought to Joharah was not of its chill. During that time of shorter periods of sunlight that was somehow not as warm and was accompanied by more rain that was also more chill, many words were said to her. Too many concerned the doubtless chill of her bed and the poorness of her fire on those nights when fire was necessary. Anguish followed and behind it lurked misery, like a roc above an untended child. Lurking, waiting to pounce and overwhelm her. She staved it off. Sai was her friend. It seemed to Joharah that only Sai was her friend. Her mother tried. But her mother had never been her friend.

That Zamhar'seemed years in passage and was colder than any, though the hard film developed on water only twice, all season. Only a portion of the lengthy misery was environmental; the rest existed within Joharah's mind.

She made fire when others did not, and kept it banked, and was laughed and whispered about. Both Shuhalan Frogsnout and Azar Hizar's son importuned her. And only one meant marriage! She felt that call that women feel, and she knew misery and need. But she did not submit to it or to those men. She abode, while the Cooling filled her bones and her soul with chill. She was childless widow of one and betrothed to another, who was not here.

Feeling weak, staggered and nigh to yielding, she nevertheless coped and abode. She remained strong or nearly, even during periods of paralyzing despair and dysphoria as miasmic as the swamps wherein dragons and leeches lurked. She wept and slept in the dark and awoke to the chill of that long darkness of too much rain, for such was their curse for not being perfect in the eyes of Allah. (Of al-Bah'ram!) Slim and young and more attractive than she thought, Joharah existed. Existing was coping.

Somehow she was able to continue to see the situation as challenge, as finite, not as threat unto destruction. Stress, Lazarus had said, resulted when the experiencer perceived the demands of the environment as being beyond her resources to cope. Joharah's perceptions never went quite that far, never quite across the line into despair. She coped.

And the sun began to rise earlier to bring the Warming again upon the world, with rain and steaming forest and swamp and a rainbow of upsurging, upleaping fungi and lichen, vines and blossoms. The season of heat followed. The reality of her situation did not change, but the environment ceased being a part of the problem.

Joharah remained well inside herself. There was shelter there, of a sort. Still Raaf Saurslayer did not return, as the brighter season deepened. She felt that she was ugly and skinny and worthless before man and God. Others, mainly young women, were pleased to aid her in feeling so.

("Doesn't that make you feel important," Sai said after his strange "all Kwait" statement, and her "No" was swift and without thought; almost an autonomic response. Hers was a reality she could not change herself. She resorted to emotion-focused or cognitive means of abiding, but she did not really believe those things she told herself.)

Raafar was enslaved by those beasts of Hajarazad; the people-hunters, some said.

The Saurslayer was slain by those Hajars, others said, for how could such a mighty hunter be enslaved, or even slain by any of the normal means that slew others?

He was slain, others said darkly (delightedly?) by the very Kingsaur he sought to attack and kill as wedding gift. Slain and eaten!

Irrationally that hypothesis was accepted and Joharah blamed. Convinced of her worthlessness without knowing why, she accepted that as part of her great load, and her mind bowed the more. The situation enshrouded and owned her, but she was not able to change it. She must wait, and she waited. She abode. Her waiting for him, her expectation of his return despite the passage of so much time, was part of her coping, an artful ambiguity that enabled her to avoid collapse.

The season of heat was little better for her than the Cooling. Depression was her companion far more than Sai. She saw to her own unhappiness, by her own thoughts, and yet she fought stress. Others saw to it that unhappiness festered into misery, by their words and their jibes. Though she must abide there, Kwait was no longer her home.

She was accursed and she knew it. Her father was no solace to one who brought disaster on men and on himself. How could he be? He was a man, a father. A father must be at once Kingsaur and guardian but never friend or confidante. Her mother knew her troubles, and she was a woman. Yet she was no solace *because* she was a woman. Joharah watched suspicion of her come upon their minds like clouds darkening the sky. They had decided that she was accursed; that she was a curse to men. She believed it and yet told herself that she did not.

Joharah wallowed deep, miserable and knowing that she was accursed. Only Sai truly befriended her. He was gentle, this teller of tales who was so in-turned and yet so empathetic. He talked, and she listened. She thought. She cogitated and reflected and mused, considered and weighed. And she found herself wanting. Rationality was no companion of self-pity and depression. Avoiding it was one more means of coping. Strangely, they talked, and she made suggestions and he accepted several. A man!

Something clicked inside her head, as though God had found and pushed a button marked Intellectual Stimulus/Awakening. After that she became even more Different. And more. Social design taught women dependence. Happiness and worth lay in men. Joharah . . . deviated.

Others thought of Sai as tale-teller, a thing, and found him attractive for that reason, or at least interesting. To Joharah he was interesting and then attractive as Sai, because he was Sai. It was almost as if he needed her. And Raafar did not return.

The season of heat became summer and Ramadan loomed. Tayruz approached her father, though by then she was drawn and thin and fit company for none.

"No. She is mate-promised to Raafar

Saurslayer. Do not think of it, Tayruz son of Sakh't."

"He is dead."

"No. He will return to claim his woman. What if he finds you then, mated with her he sought Kingsaur for?"

"I will hold and protect her. If necessary, I will kill him!"

Her father laughed. That ended Tayruz's suit. He went to the father of fat-chested Shamsah, and soon they were betrothed. He made no rash promises as to bride-gift, and Shamsah had a husband, and worth.

Johara waited, a prisoner of depression. At times death seemed a haven long awaited and to be desired. She was a woman, a new-woman in her prime. She should have been mother, bright as a bloom of the phosphorescent fungus *spirt*, and all knew it. Instead she was again called maiden, though she was not and it was insulting, and she was alone, alone. It was not possible for her to pass so into another Zamhar'. She found herself longing for Sai. Aye, even Sai Tale-teller!

She did abide. A coper, she did pass through Ramadan the interminable, and then another Cooling. Long and long that Zamhar' was. She gained back none of the weight she had lost during the fasting of Ramadan. Others, miserable, ate in attempt to ease the misery, and thereby increased it. Joharah, in misery, did not eat. The fat puffy side of a shieldhood mushroom, and the thin-vaned underside. In the dark, ever in the dark, even when the sun was bright.

That Cooling passed, and Raafar Saurslayer returned to Kwait.

With him came no happiness for Joharah.

From afar, he was magnificent as he approached. Hugely tall, yet so muscular as to appear stocky. The shield on his back shadowed his head, above which thrust the long point of his spear.

"A new spear," Akal observed. None questioned, for a proud father knew his son's spear.

Raafar came nearer and his head seemed to glow, as though God and sun smiled on this great hunter among hunters. A child broke from its parent and ran out to meet him, squealing happily. It stopped well short, as if struck, and stared, and turned to come back at the run. Now it screamed, rather than squealed. He clutched his mother's thighs and looked fearfully back as if the approaching man were the Kingsaur he had fared forth to slay. And Raaf came on, returning to Kwait, and Johara felt faint with relief and welling happiness.

Oh, they will not chide me or sneer at me tomorrow . . .

And then he was close enough so that his face was distinguishable. The gleam on the left side of his head could not be denied. And now neither could the rest of it.

The gleam was the sunlight on bare skull, shining lurid pink and seamed with horrid cicatrices. No hair grew there, left of the midline of his skull. Dreadful tearing claws had torn away scalp and hair so that only hideous, shining scar tissue remained. One ran down his forehead, and farther. Gone was that smooth and noble hunter's brow. and gone was the left eye of Raafar Saurslayer.

Still Joharah felt faint, but no longer from relief and joy. Now her stomach lurched and she stared in horror. Accursed! Accursed!

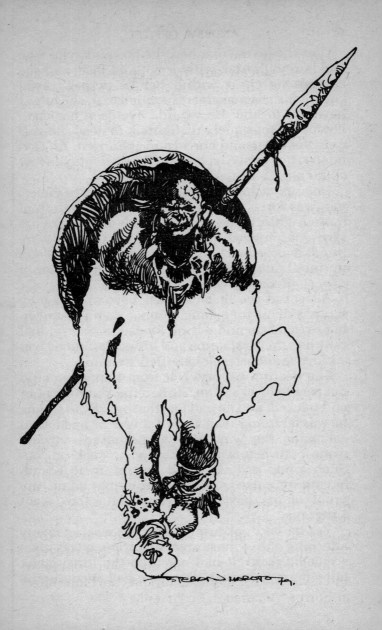

Had she loved him; had she been his wife who had lain with him, with or without love; had she carried his child within her or perhaps even known his passion and responded to it, she might have run to him. He would have been her man, however grotesquely disfigured. Instead, he was only the latter, and horrid and abhorrent. Ah God no, no, not this! She had suffered so much! How could she deserve this?

He approached, and there was more. His nose, too, was torn. The healing—rather, formation of those frightful scars with so much drawing of the skin—had tugged it up so that the nostrils were lifted, exposed as two holes that one had to look up into. Part of the upper lip was gone, too, to expose those big white, white teeth.

All could see that he must have spent many months of his long, long absence merely recovering so that he could return. Raafar Saurslayer had returned, in his stamina and his pride, and he was a hideous monster. Johara fled weeping.

She heard the story. Not from him; she could not bear to be near him. He had tracked Kingsaur, and tracked, and he had lost that one. By that time he was far from Kwait, and of course he had had to eat along the way. Having promised—vowed, made oath before God—he had to seek on, on. Such a one as Raaf could not return to Kwait, having promised, without bringing home the proof of his having met and slain the tyrant Kingsaur.

Yet he had not been mutilated while bravely attacking one of those erect monsters. It was none so magnificent. It had not been the three-meter tall Kingsaur on its two legs he had encountered and battled. It had been a swamp dragon. The alligator big enough to swallow a big man at a single gulp. Formidable, aye. Yet he had not attacked it; the creature had taken him ignominiously by surprise, while he slept. He slept with a full belly, confident and supreme, for he had slain a spotcat over a meter tall at the shoulder, and had now its hide as cloak or blanket for the Cooling, tail and all. Like a sated beast Raaf had lain up at swamp's edge, safe from twinerbitch and spiculdag, shaded by a great twisty grandfather spidertree festooned with dribblechin. When the usually timid monster lurched up out of the swamp with murky water running off its scales, Raaf had time only to roll whirling aside and lay hand on spear. He could have fled, then. He was Raafar Saurslayer, and he did not.

He pounced up and whirled to drive centimeter after centimeter of spearhead into the obscenely pink-white underbelly of the swamp dragon. And out, straining, and in again. Again, straining and stabbing there at water's edge . . .

He had slain it, he said. All the while, it had tried to bite off his head. Teeth long as his fingers had scraped all along one side, face and scalp, and yet he had continued to stab and twist until it sagged and fell onto its back. He had sunk down too, knowing he had slain it and thinking it had slain him; thinking to bleed to death. Because he was Raafar Saurslayer he had instead dragged himself, prone, to a clumpy spray of that anticoagulant lichen called grapnel. Having plastered his wounds with it, he passed out.

He should have died. Yet surely God was favoring him, for nothing came to eat or entwine him

and, with attendant agony, his wounds fought to heal. In the next periods and days and weeks he had awakened and passed out again and again. He should have died. Because he was Raafar Saurslayer, he had not. He had healed himself, alone, Hideously, in agony, he had healed himself, and was hideous in result. And he returned. Hideous. A grotesque monster of a man. He had not slain a Kingsaur. Because he was Raafar Saurslayer, he said that he would, and vowed it anew.

Desperate, Joharah hit on that very promise. She called it vow, pointed out that it had not been kept, and mentioned honor, hers and his and her father's. (Her father would not uphold her in that. He showed shock. Her mother was a woman and understood. But she was married to Joharah's father, and she too expressed shock at her daughter's attempt to avoid mating with Raafar.) As she did: therefore, Joharah said, she considered their betrothal invalidated, abdicated from by Raaf. She said that she would not marry him.

She could not see happiness at the end of such a road, but surely what would come would be better than having to spend all her days with that horror she did not love and now could never love. Better the loneliness and depression that had already been her close companions for so long.

It was not enough. Many were horrified not by Raaf but by her overweening self interest—or professed to be, for people could be cruelly moral and smug when their own lives were not involved. Among them were his father and Raafar himself. He knew how he looked and yet said that thought of Joharah—"his" Joharah—had sustained him, enabled him to survive. Ah, that was pain and damnation, that statement that made her appear villainous and without heart! And then, shock upon shock, her father disavowed what she had said, and declared himself more than satisfied of his honor, and hers, and Raaf's, and honored the betrothal as he honored the man who had given up so much in his attempt to present his bride with a gift to transcend all others.

No one mentioned Raafar's overweening pride, not now.

And now, now, she who had waited long and long waited yet again. This time Sai was with her, making marks in the ground with a shining sabretooth and pointing out that "all Kwait held its breath" in awaiting the announcement. She and Raaf had had no meeting, because she refused to face that horror he had become.

Marry that! Call that mate! Lie with that, serve it, look at it day after day and night after night; bear its children. No!

Judgment must be made. She had no choice but to submit to that. She, the Speaker of Judgments, ate of the God-things and went alone to await enlightenment. With the God on her, and his Lion on her. And so . . . all Kwait held its breath. And Joharah waited, and waited.

"She comes," Sai said of a sudden, low of voice, for Joharah was not looking.

She did not want to look, now. She did. The Speaker of Judgments came forth in the twilight. They had heard her shrieking and moaning in the throes of receiving the God-guidance. Now she seemed slumped, in a depressive state, tiny and as if sad beneath the great maned head of the Lion of

God. She wore the barest minimum otherwise, and no gaudery, and the hide of that enormous Lion slain by the father of the father of the Leader. Some said it was the last lion. No one had ever seen another.

With many words, the Speaker of Judgments told all Kwait that Raafar Saurslayer had essayed, and striven on behalf of his bride-to-be, and had paid a terrible penalty. She pointed out that Joharah had been glad enough to be his betrothed, and had not stipulated the slaying of a Kingsaur as her bride-gift. Now, "because the mighty hunter and pride of Kwait Raafar son of Akal is sore wounded unto disfigurement and no longer the handsomest of men, Joharah finds cause to reject him as mate."

Listening to her name pronounced so formally with the throaty gasp at the end, hearing the words and their chosen tenor, Joharah knew what was coming. She stared at the strange felino-human in the twilight, but she no longer saw. She felt heavy, and hot, doomed and damned, and she considered with a brain that rushed like water downhill into the swamp.

Banishment would have meant going alone from Kwait, into a forest filled with the giant saurs—"terrible lizards" or dinosaurs—and long-tooths and other horrors. It was surely a sentence of death. A Judgment in her favor would surely condemn her to more loneliness, followed—doubtless after a long while—either by marriage to some lesser man or still more loneliness and depression unto death. As rendered and now spoken, the Judgment was life in Kwait: if she could live as mate to the mightiest hunter of

Kwait: For that was the Judgment. The marriage was to take place. Joharah sat slumped, seeing nothing.

The long night came, and darkrain. Johara had time to ponder, to commiserate with herself without being on view. She pondered long, and tried to consider all that might befall. Although that was not possible and she could not be said to be fully rational, she decided. This time she could act to change her situation. She did. She rejected the Judgment, which was a known horror. She chose the unknown one of banishment: flight.

Most secretively, Sai aided her. She fled Kwait, and Raafar and all she knew and hated.

She embraced instead all that they all feared—except that she feared Raafar more.

She fled alone, in the rain, determined to keep moving until she dropped, that she would be far and far before she was missed. Alone. At night, under the cold and uncaring moons. Oddly, there was a new Something in the sky. Was it a sign? If so, did it portend good or continued ill for her? She did not know, and wondered if that new Something in the sky, so tiny and yet new, and there; wondered if it had a name.

6

Year 73: Today the Big Rain fell on Jauhar!—
is falling still! A water table is forming on this
'new' world. It begins! The Bah'ram made the
announcement in his strong voice. It does
inspire confidence. It could be the voice of
Mahomet, returned . . .

> —journal of Meh'met al-Habees,
> Station Jauhar

"Tell me about your name."

She sighed, stretched, and made a yawny noise.
"I made it up," she said, lying supine beside him.
"I mean, I adopted it. 'Cicada' was the name of one
of the people in a book by . . . I forgot. No I don't;
a book by R.F. Barton. It—"

"Burton?"

"What?"

"R.F. Burton," Allayth said. "Richard Frankis
Burton."

"No no, smarty. Barton. No name given, just
initials R.F. and the name, and more initials:
Scholar letters. R.F. Barton. The book was *Autobiographies of Three Pagans*. One of those
pioneer sociological works from back in the early
twentieth century, pre-technology. The days of
Mead and Ellis and Malinowksi and Radin—just
before Transition. And Freud, of course. Barton

actually went to this island, Ifu—no no, the
Philippines. The people were a tribe called the
Ifugao. Primitives."

"Naked?"

She smiled, remembering their conversation
about nudity and the reasons for clothing. "Not
quite. Missionaries had already got to them. Anyhow, Cicada is the name of a woman in that book.
She was young and happy and then she became a
figure of real tragedy and then she was dead."

"Tragic?"

"She was murdered by her husband. Stabbed."

He rubbed her leg, very bare and very smooth.
"That's tragic. Men had all the rights among the
primitives, didn't they. Marry him your father
agreed with, and be his chattel and slave, and be
replaced by a clap of the hands and a few words.
Or murder. Well. A strange name then—but not
tragic for you, Cicada! So this primitive of long,
long ago had the name of an extinct insect and you
liked it and took it. That isn't tragic, that's romantic. What was your name?"

"I'm not going to tell you." Cicada giggled. It
was strange, her girlish giggle. She was older than
he, by five years. And giggled. "I didn't know it
was the name of an extinct insect until after I had
read the book and taken the name."

He smiled. Filling in time. Spaceships should
have nice murals above the bunks, he thought,
staring upward. Filling in time. Talking, being
close and delight-sharing *apreś-sexe;* studiously
not talking about It. Space Station Mausoleum:
the Orbiting Mausoleum of Jauhar al-Ajr: It. He
realized what she had said. "Read the book? You
said read?"

"The real book! Yes! I *saw* it! Its cover was green and gold. Vertically bisected into the two colors."

"Ugh. You're poking my eye."

"No no, I'm serious. I did see it. On microspool I mean, of course."

"Of course."

"But I saw it, and full-sized, too, even the old binding. Green and gold," she repeated dreamily. "The photographs. Flat, and in shades of gray only. I've had an order in for that book for *years*. I'll never get it. Anyhow. I am Cicada. After an Ifugao, not an insect. She was very happy, for a long time." She thumped his chest, lying on her back beside him. "Do *not* call me Locust. Or Bug!"

"I'll try to remember. I wouldn't have thought of it if you hadn't reminded me. Couldn't think of the other name for a 'cicada.'' Lurie is your name?"

"Of course, Jimajin."

He felt her twitching in a silent giggle. "I've never heard it either. It's a pretty name. What I meant was, did you make it up—adopt it, too?"

She let the giggle out. "Yes!"

"Oh—Allison Lurie!"

"Wrong. I thought it was pretty too, by the way, and still do. I like my name. Everyone should choose its own name. No, it's for Nancy Lurie. She wrote *Mountain Wolf Woman, Sister of Crashing Thunder*—isn't that a marvelous name? A real name, of a Northamerican Indian."

"A little long," he said smiling, and was thumped in the ribs.

"Another real book," Cicada said. "She also wrote the introduction to *Autobiographies of Three Pagans*."

"You really love that book!"

"I really do. It's the most fascinating book I ever read. It's *real*, a real book about real people, I mean. A major contribution to sociological knowledge. Even in nineteen . . . nineteen . . . whenever it was that Barton was there, the Ifugao people were alien. Alien! The way the Americans were to the Japanese, in that war that began technology and the Transition Era. The way the Japanese were to *everyone* of the west! The Arabs were alien to the west too, in the twenty-first when they achieved ascendancy. Your ancestors! Alien, alien! That book *made* me become a sociologist, Jimajin; an exosociologist."

Staring at the ceiling, feeling good, talking about herself and the happy past when there were primitives one could go off and study, she toyed idly with one lobe of her chest. She would not be a problem to herself, running bare-chested.

"Is that the real color of your eyes? The original color, I mean."

"Yes. Oh I had them green for a while; several years in fact. It was fun. We all play around that way, don't we? Can you imagine what it would have been like if the neo-revisionist Muslims had won out, with all those austere rules?"

"Ugh. Save us from that old concept of Allah and his anti-everything Prophet, may his tribe decrease."

"Right. My name though—I'm glad I did that. I am Cicada Lurie, by the grace of me, and so I stay until death doth me and my name part! You wear the name you were born with?"

"Yuh. Uh . . . Cicada? What are your secret fantasies? Sexual fantasies?"

He was sure he felt a little tension in the thigh against his, and he was surprised when she answered after only a few seconds. "Oh, being queen or something. Tying up a man and having him at my mercy. My slave, you know."

"Sex slave."

"Of course. What's your secret phantasy?"

He sighed. "Good old Freud. About the same as yours, only the other way around."

"Oh." After a while she added, "Well, we're not too complementary there, are we? Maybe we'll have to think about it. Maybe a trade-off? I just don't know. I still don't know about lots of things, Jimajin Allayth." Another little silence hovered, pregnant to bursting. Just as he got ready to throw words out, almost desperately, she spoke again. "Jim. What do we do now? Nudge the Mausoleum and let it dive into Jauhar al-Ajr to cremate all the dust of all those poor centuries-old smears?"

He felt her shudder when she said that. Their hips were touching. Hers were lean, but female lean—oh definitely female. "Go down to see what's there?"

He squeezed his eyes shut, blotting out too-low ceiling—a comforting cloud-strewn slate blue— and concentrated on assimilating, on setting his mental wheels into new tracks. (Shifting gears, he thought fleetingly; he who had studied the past and even toyed with the idea of it, some of it, participating in the revival of the Society for Creative Anachronism. The past was always better.)

He opened his eyes and his mouth and avoided answering for a few seconds longer: "We've been doing a very good job of not talking about that, Cicada."

"I know. But not of not-thinking about it. Have we." It wasn't really a question. To answer would be cowardly, a continuing avoidance. She started to turn onto her side against him, front against side, and decided against it. It could be a distraction and thus an excuse, for both of them.

He said, "No. We haven't succeeded in not-thinking. God!"

She echoed him: "*Allah!*" And she added, "Yes. God." This time pronouncing it the other way, the old Inglisi way, in one syllable with its two hard consonants. How soft was the name of the god of warriors, with its pair of 1's and *a*'s and the terminal "ah!"

He sighed. Felt his heartbeat step up, in apprehension, not anticipation. He got the words out: "I think we must move. Get up I mean. Cleanse. Shave."

"No, thanks. Maybe, possibly you have noticed my cellular readjustment: no hair below the face."

"Die young," he said, as earlier members of his kind had said "Drop dead;" a ritual known to sociologists. Meaningless. Mere words. He recognized that this time she had slithered off the subject. The subject was What To Do, and they were the only people around to decide. He wished for Flaerti. Good old calm old, *old* wise father-image Senior Scholar Flaerti. "And eat," he said determinedly. Leading. "Then we should dictate. Separately. Record everything we saw and touched and felt and said."

"Everything?" Her voice had gone a bit squeaky. That reminded him to hang onto his.

"Die young, rotten b—" He stopped. He would not call her bug. He would never have thought of it, and wished now that she had not mentioned it. *Insect, maybe,* he afterthought, and controlled his grin. The subject. The subject. Reality. Now. It—the Mausoleum. That was now. That and

Jauhar al-Ajr: Jewel of Heaven. A bright, flashing, pendent jewel, swinging scintillantly along through the heaven it brightened, accompanied by three pearls . . . and surrounded by massive, horrible death. Ancient death. The sort of death a man in the position Allayth had so long occupied could forget happened: violent death. Murder.

She squeezed his thigh and Allayth twitched a little. He was ticklish just above the knee, the same as others were on their soles. He could not bear a real squeeze there. Hers was small and brief and he withstood it with only a twitch.

"I don't want to separate," Cicada said in a most uncharacteristically small voice, and she did not sound like a woman who fancied tying a man to possess and tease him. "Not . . . not after what we . . . saw." Again he felt her shudder.

"I don't either," he said, hardly feeling worthy of tying up anyone and making it his slave. It might be nice to be a slave, right now. That way someone else would be making the decisions. "I don't either," he said. "The tapes we make will be important, Cicada. Important documents, I mean. We are scientists. Let's go be scientific."

"Then what?"

She is pushing me to decide, he thought. *Maybe we should both just run, find someone to decide for us. Is that what everyone wants? A Living God, right there at hand. Do this and do that, and *I* shall see to the rest, little mortals!*

"Then what? Then, uh, lunch. Come on, Cicada. *Then* we can think about what we do next. Right now I've found some fine scientific reasons to put off deciding or even thinking about it. Up up up!"

"Jim." She had not moved either.

"Yuh?"

"We should input the computer with everything. It can tell us, uh, give us an indication of what to do. Can't it?"

He sighed. "I'll tell you what it will tell us—I mean 'indicate what we must do.' "

"Oh Jimajin, don't."

"What we have to do is suit up again and go back into the Mausoleum and search. We have to—"

"Oh God."

"—to find records. Individual journals, diaries, logs, anything. Everything they recorded. And bring it back here."

"Oh God. I was afraid you'd say that."

"No, you knew that one of us would say it, sooner or later. You just made *me* say it, Cicada. It's what we have to do." *And after that,* he was thinking, *we would be stupid not to go down on-planet. Foolish to do it—but stupid not to!* "We have to try to find out who murdered the space station, and why."

"I know. I don't feel . . . scientific or decisive. I feel very . . . uh, what used to be called female."

He did not chuckle. He heard nothing humorous. He understood. First he sucked in a long, long breath and let it out long. Next he rose slowly to a sitting position, vampire style. Good for the stomach. He had a pretty good stomach—he was in pretty good shape, in point of fact. As Cicada was.

"I don't feel scientific either, Cicada. If you mean you wish your heart would slow down and you sort of want a nice convenient god or a father or a nice big strong male . . . so do I." And he made the effort, and got up.

7

Year 75: Analysis of all sensor reports now proves that there are no native microorganisms on Jauhar al-Ajr. As we planned! Tomorrow we begin seeding the 'new' planet's new nitrogen-oxygen atm. with our own Terran bacteria . . .
                              —journal of Abdullah Khatib, on
                                          Station Jauhar

She could not understand why the men of Hajarazad had not used her. To be taken by them was horrifying and it was horror, and yet she accepted. Her choice did not exist. Too, had it not been shown her again and again that she was accursed, damned? She remained petrified of their leader. Abdur was a beast, a squat ugly creature less than human. It pleased God and Bah'ram to make such, occasionally. It was hard not to question; to wonder why. Still, he did not try to embrace her, and she accepted captivity. Had it not been shown her again and again that she was not her own, that no worth existed in her?

Less than a day—two sleeps, though she hardly slept—after she fled Kwait, they had surprised and easily taken her. How briefly she had known freedom! Now she was captive of the men of Hajarazad, land of unpleasant legend.

The collar was heavy and the chains clinked when she moved. The sound of the bronze links was as constant as the noise of the forest.

If she faltered she was snarled at or her chain dragged taut so that she must hurry, or turn, or stop, as they wished. The alternative was pain to her neck from the heavy collar, and a threat to her breathing. That was a constant renewed source of terror. To the collar were secured long slim chains. The one in front served as her leash and lead, so that she hurried when necessary and turned when that was indicated. She adapted swiftly, and avoided stumbling. The chain attached to the back of her collar reminded her to stop. It also caught her hair and became entangled in it. That brought the swift sharp pain that seemed to squeeze forth tears and to hurt as much as a splinter under a nail.

She strove to be swiftly obedient to commands and tugs, and not to fall. She tried not to cry out. And she wondered why she had not been used. Had she lost attractiveness, with so much loss of weight? (She had been quite plump, once.) She had no wish to be used by them. It was just that she was unable not to wonder.

They had come upon her when she had fought her way through the forest for many hours, many many hours. Through a sleep and a period and another sleep. She had hurried but never run—so as not to fall, and so as to avoid betraying herself to hungry beasts. Even so she had narrowly avoided blundering into a knee-high growth of puffballs, and she had nearly hanged herself on a loop of jumpvine thick as her wrist, slung from a tree a hundred meters and more in height. At last in that maze of boles and dense growth of lesser flora, she had collapsed in weariness and her last memory was of the twitching of her legs.

This time she was fortunate, for nothing discovered her while she slept. No beast so much as awoke her. Sleep was a haven and a blanket that enveloped her. Yet in that sleep was Raafar. Poor, hideous Raafar. The dreams were probably the result of feasting insects.

Even soundly as she slept, she had cried out at her dreams. A fellow captive told her so, later. That was how they had found her. So she had betrayed herself into captivity. Yet how could she have slept peacefully, even in her weariness? She had fled Kwait, her own people, her whole life. All in horror of Raafar.

She awoke to find the men standing all about her. They were staring at her, and they were strangers. Every one wore the sandals and disk-armlet of Hajarazad. All trace and tendril of sleep fled her in an eye's blink. Yet she did not cry out, not even at the squat hideousness of their leader. To what purpose, an outcry? She merely stared at them. Conscious of a full bladder; conscious of itches; the various marks of twigs and other things on which she'd lain, and ticks from the big dead tree. She did not scratch. She rose partway to a sitting position, arms propping her, and she stared.

"You are ours. Try to flee and we will bring you down. Resist and you will be overpowered and I will be careful to beat your fruits. We do not want your gauds or your clothing. We want you, and we have you. What is your village?"

"Kwait."

She heard herself make that reply, and heard that her voice was tiny and quavered. So brief her freedom! From horror into terror into captivity.

"K'wait," one of them said, pronouncing it wrong.

"How far is it?"

"I . . . I do not know—"

He looked mean. That was easy for him, an ugly, bandy-legged, mean-looking man. One of the beast-men, or nearly. Hideous. *And I fled Raafar! Dakhilak ya Bah'ram!*—under thy protection, O Bahram! She glanced down from him, and saw marks on her from the insects and the forest detritus she had lain on.

"I left at firstdark. I am sure I have walked through two sleeps." She blinked. Even in the forest, the sun penetrated, and it was bright. The measure of her freedom was one night. When the beastly man continued to stare, she added hastily, "—and a period. Then I—I collapsed."

He cocked his head. "You must be fleeing this Kwait! Now you know that you should have stayed, eh? Eh? Bare one fruit. You choose which, and do it quickly. How far is Kwait?"

She looked about her, blinking. She saw only the boles of trees, and fungus in its myriad shapes and sizes, and grasses and vines that were like braces seemingly propping some trees and like serpents that climbed others, enwrapping. And she saw men. There were eight. Seven spears, eight daggers, five shields, five swords, eight armlets of disks, and a whip. Ugly faces, ugly hair, terrifying teeth. Beasts. They were not of her people; they were beasts.

In the forest, a great saur bellowed. A big sweat-sucker landed on the leader's forearm and he sent

it flying with a ripple of his skin. The saur blasted forth its call again. It was far off.

"I—I do not know! I just . . . just . . . fled!"

"Ha! Which way is Kwait from here?"

Again she did not know, and she said so. She had known before she collapsed into sleep, or thought she did. Now she was unsure. Perhaps she could ascertain the direction. Yet it was easy for them to see the way she had come. Hunters saw such things.

"You know little indeed, little *kahbah* of Kwait! What did I tell you to do?"

She remembered, and yet she heard his word, and hated it. Without her full volition, someone in her answered angrily.

"I am no whore! And I will not bare my breast for you!"

He drew his dagger. "Then I will bare both of them, and see a bit of blood too for my trouble!"

Trying very hard to look contemptuous rather than fearful, she tugged the softened hide of the spotcat away from one shoulder. Somewhere, far above the trees, a pterosaur scrawked.

"Mabahr: cut that strap. Hold your grin, and do not touch her. Be still, girl of Kwait. No kahbah, eh eh? You slept alone all through the Cooling?"

"I did!"

She did not deign to glance sidewise at him called Mabahr, whose knife was sharp. Her right shoulder strap was sliced swiftly through and she would not re-cover her chest without tying a knot. She sat before them with one breast bare and atremble. That its bareness felt good was not good.

"You are not mated?"

"No."

"Ah."

He looked about at his companions and his glance seemed full of significance. She wished that she were ugly, she who knew that she was not despite her being wedded to self-denigration. Standing males, all towering so male-ly over the ground-seated, semi-reclining female they had surprised.

"Tohfah," he said; a choice gift. His eyes swept back and his gaze was a black knife that stabbed her. "You are ours. You will be collared—Saryd! You will wear chain. Our chain. In that is security. With us is safety from . . . whoever?—you fled in . . . Kwait. Kwait? Yes. You fled alone and were in danger from any predator, eh? Eh? Now you go with us, safe from all, for we are of Hajarazad, and mighty. Stand up, and be still while a collar is put upon you."

"Lah," she said sadly. "Do not do this."

He returned to his fixation: "Yes. We do. The alternative is simple, and I would enjoy it: we skewer those pretty fruits and lead you thus. Stand."

She stood. Her little "uh" came from the tug of the strained lifter-puller muscles down the fronts of her thighs. She was collared. She received the two chains, while several of the men of the Hajarazad took counsel quietly. Twice she heard the word "Kwait," and saw their glances. Her track back through the forest was indicated by a pointing finger. Did Kwait lie in that direction?

Of course not. How could she have moved in a straight line, in the rain, through the tropical forest? Tons of refuse fell from it daily to soften and enrich the ground. In some places it was piled, or a tree had fallen and at last been released by vines, or the huge mother-root of a vine knotted up above the ground like a great boil, spewing its scion roots that lofted on trees. Or stinger mushrooms spread for a meter or more and must be avoided, or gigantic puffballs threatened to release their green gas if so much as touched. She remembered half-circling the bole of a ginkcoid tree that must have been ten times thicker than she. She remembered skirting a magenta morel whose stem was thicker than her thigh and whose canopy, just over a meter off the ground, must be well over two meters in diameter. She remembered turning aside—dashing aside, heart pounding!—from a serpent thick as her ankle—except where it bulged to thigh thickness with whatever had been its recent prey. It had not been at all interested in her, but she had not known, at first.

Somehow, they agreed on a direction in which they thought Kwait lay.

With her unused, untouched, and with one lobe of her chest denuded and bothersomely bobbling, they headed away from that direction. Toward Hajarazad? She supposed; she supposed. With an acceptance of kismet that was beyond insouciance, she supposed. And went.

She could not understand why they had not used her. Had she lost so much weight that she was no longer attractive even to captors, even for rape?

She was willing to believe it.

I would have to look up to meet the eyes of a snake, she thought, and was led, collared captive, through the forest. Her fellow captives were three, left with four others of Hajarazad when eight came to find the source of her dream-cries. All the three captives were male. None was of Kwait. One was naked, and limped. They too were chained. More than she, for their wrists were connected by long lengths of clinking links.

The people of Kwait were proud to take no slaves, she thought with some pride.

Unless they chanced upon a lone outlander— meaning anyone not of Kwait—whose taking was irresistibly easy and surely fated. Pride came from the fact that Kwait sought no slaves.

Obviously, Hajarazad sought slaves.

Wives? she wondered. Then why men? Workers? Then why a woman?

They ate mushrooms, meatplant when it presented itself. A threehorn fled them. Many serpents did. One, huge, did not and was killed. The men of Hajarazad disdained its meat, which Johara knew was good. These weird men with their bestial leader—were they no hunters? Were they hunters only of humans? She entertained a pleasant disdain until she remembered. She was no longer of Kwait. She had fled Raafar, and so Kwait. She was slaved.

A fellow slave liked her, one of those with clothing. In truth he was well favored. He was also younger than she, she felt, and after all, a slave. She disdained him, though she saw that he liked her and wanted her. Only a slave, she mused. *What is it to be desired by a slave?*

She *felt* his eyes, hot and soft all at once under long lashes. A pretty boy, she thought. Soft and pretty, with soft black eyes and sensuous lips. A slave.

Tired of walking, they slept. Despite the con-

stant noises of various saurs, Terrible Lizards,
they slept. The captives slept chained. She knew
the screamy roar she heard was either a spotcat or
a daggertooth. She was sure that her captors knew
which. Yet, spotcat or tiger, chains or no, she and
the others slept. In chains. They lay down in
sunlight—such that filtered down amid the
foliage—and slept in sunlight and awoke in sunlight.

The rushing Thing fell from the sky shortly
after she awoke. Led, she gazed up at it. Someone
exclaimed and pointed. It was not a pterosaur and
it gleamed like metal. Yet she knew it had to be
alive; it was too large for any spore, and it flew.
She thought she saw stubby wings and perhaps
teeth, but she was sure the wings never flapped.
Yet it had to be alive. How else could it slow so
much, and maneuver, before disappearing into

the forest far ahead? It *was* far; they heard no sound and no impact. It was not something that had fallen and while she wondered, so did the men of Hajarazad. They talked about it, wondering, opining. The people-hunters of Hajarazad paused to take quiet counsel again, with gesticulating and much rolling of eyes and twitching while they discussed that which had fallen or soared from the sky and was no pterosaur and not King Dragon either. She heard them say "roc" several times—rukh, which was the flying serpent, the pterosaur. It had flown the sky, descending, and it had definitely come to alight, not fallen.

After awhile they went on. Moving in the direction of it or It. Cooler heads had prevailed. But wiser ones? She wondered. And plodded on, chained, clinking.

JAUHAR AL-AJR
summary of data

Jauhar

Mass _____ _____10^{18} kg (5.18 quintillion)

density _____ 5.19 g/cm³ (slightly less than Earth's)

Diameter _____ 1.24 x 10⁴ km (12,400 km)

surface gravity _____ 0.92 Earth

Distance from primary _____ 155 million km

length of year _____ 391 Terran days
73.3

Rotation [day] _____ 128 hours

Satellites

	km distance	g mass	km diameter	g/cm³ density
#1	9,990	4.169 x 10²¹	174.4	1.5
#2	17,704	2.124 x 10²⁰	51.3	3.0
#3	392,270	2.38 x 10¹⁶	11.26	5.3

	period of revolution Jauharan days	inclination degrees N of equator	apparent size
#1	5.25 hr.	2	1°
#2	6.99 hr.	3	10′
#3	5.7 hr.	72° retrograde	point

Notes

Moons 1 and 2, despite similarity in their planes of orbit, rarely eclipse each other: Their orbits precess around the planet. Sun and both moons rise in W. and set in E.
#3 is retrograde; rises as a bright star in NE and sets in SW. It is a point of light; bright, with no visible disc.

#1 is twice the size of *Luna*; #2 is 1/3 *Luna's* size.

Climate on planet Jauhar al-Ajr

The long day creates extremes in temperature: hotter days, colder nights.

Temperate zones are dense tropical rain forests, while equatorial regions are deserts. Rain falls just after sunrise and just after sunset. Heat under forest canopy keeps temperature well above freezing; temp. reaches 38 C°[101F] by day, and falls to 5–10°C at night.

WINTER: "The Cooling" lasts ¼ year as on Earth, or about 25 Jauharan days. Characterized by rainfall during day and night with temperatures reaching only 21°–27°C during the day.
On one or two occasions throughout the season temp may drop to freezing at night, with only a very light frost.

8

Year 80: It is weird. Yet I must not doubt, or let anyone know my thoughts or the truth. I command in his name—His name, one is tempted to say, vocally capitalizing—and though I have heard his strong, commanding voice that so inspires confidence, *I have never seen him!* I! It is incredible; al-Bah'ram must by now be far over a hundred years old.

—21 Rashad Pazechki, Station Jauhar;
commanding

Cygnet was a small jumpship and not armed; why should it be? Space piracy was buried with Killer Kane of Buck Rogers—and with Chinchem Falthom, who had actually tried it. Briefly. It had not paid. While it could not be said that Earth now had no enemies, there were no open hostilities. The last real "incident" lay forty-seven Terran years in past: one spaceship destroyed with three hundred thirty-one people; followed by three warcraft from Earth and nineteen of Lyonesse with all crew, followed by some half the real estate and populace of a city of two millions. *Pax Terris* prevailed . . . and space war, like piracy, was just too frightfully expensive.

Reasons were cited for arming the three people aboard the little jumpship *Cygnet*. The decision,

however, was not to do. Theirs was a mission of
contact and observation: Study and learn. Unarmed, they would be far less suspect by people
who might well be xenophobically suspicious.
Unarmed, the trio from Earth would be more
likely to hold to scientific purpose and care, and
studied amicability.

"And what if *they* start something?" Cicada
Lurie had asked, back on Earth.

"Well then Lurie, we will have learned something about them. And with our emissaries unarmed, any hostilities by these . . . others will
clearly make them villains. Rest assured that in
that case we shall certainly interfere with their
culture."

"Why . . . you're deliberately setting us
up—we are considered expendable!"

"Ugly word, Lurie."

"Ugly truth!" she said with vehemence, thinking that little could be uglier than his bureaucrat's
blandness.

He did hew to honesty, though: "You are expendable, Lurie. So are Gadnason and Allayth. If
it must come to such ugly talk, so are the people
you will be visiting."

"Suppose one of us smuggles a weapon aboard
that pitifully little craft you say we must use?"

"Don't."

"We will have a repair laser, won't we?"

"Do stop thinking that way, Lurie. You sound
dangerously militant and that is not a proper scientific attitude, at all."

"One would certainly like to be able to defend
herself. If need arises, I mean."

"Avoid the need, Lurie. Be a xenosociologist,
and a diplomat."

"But—"

"What . . . else . . . Lurie?"

The world had gone all stiff and cold about then, and Cicada had closed her mouth. What else? Nothing. Onward and upward. Outward and outward. And now downward. There had been ancient weapons on the Mausoleum. One worked. Once. ("If only we hadn't tried it! We had a weapon; one good shot. Now it's dead."—"But if we hadn't tried it, we wouldn't have known we had one good shot.") Downward. Unarmed. (Repair beamer handy.) *Cygnet* gave them the information they expected. The planet had, after all, been terraformed, which meant made as Earthlike as possible.

Argon: 1.002 percent of the atmospheric composition. Carbon Dioxide: 0.0254 atm. Helium: present; forget the percentage of atm. It was present, so there were billions and billions of neutrinos zipping around all over the planet. Hydrogen: even less; fine. Krypton: no trace. Neon: 0.0026. High; so what? Nitrogen: 77.9673. Oxygen: 21.1502. Ozone and methane in trace. Xenon: absent.

"Forget inventing high-speed photography here," Allayth said. "And forget Superman, too."

"Who—oh, the Krypton absence. Is the argon level high?"

"A little. I suppose it's pretty wet down there. Lots of swamp and humidity, I mean. Twenty-one point-one-and-a-half percent of oxygen is interesting. That's a big two-tenths more than in the ship's atmosphere."

"And surely meaningless to us," Cicada said. "Ah—look, the little krypton light's flashing. There is a trace, then. A trace of a trace, anyhow."

"That's pleasant: Homey. As for the oxygen—yuh, I guess another two tenths of a percent won't make us feel giddy! It might help offset the humidity. All that green is forest, Cicada! Trees! Tropical forest, I mean. Daily rain, most likely."

"No problem for me. My sinuses wouldn't complain on a desert, or even underwater. Alien microbes?"

"No way. The A-N3 algae they used to turn this from a carbon dioxide atmosphere into a nitrogen-oxygen one were freighted with bacteria-consuming bacteria. Greedy bastards fed on anything Jauhar might have had to begin with. When they ran out of that food, they began on themselves. Our bacteria, I mean. Eating themselves. The ones riding with the blue-green algae." *You're babbling,* he told himself. *Ease off. So you're excited. No use being a fool.* "And then they died. A self-destructing strain in the simplest way: when they ran out of available food, they died, all of them. Remember that journal entry for Year 49 after the hurling of the A-N3 at the planet. It showed no trace of them. And that same year, Jauhar was 'seeded' with good old Terrene microorganisms."

"And in Year Eighty-one . . . Other Things."

"Yuh. What we are going to find are Terrene plants and bacteria. Nothing we aren't immune to. With some differences, of course. The Bah'ram was just a wee bit cracked. Hairline, say; pre-psychotic. A fanatic, and ridiculously rich. Also, the man was brilliant; no way around it. That plus his money gained him all the information and hardware he needed."

"And software," Cicada said dully.

"Not to think of the Mausoleum."

"Jim."

Cygnet bucked, sank. Twenty kilometers below sprawled Jauhar al-Ajr. Bigger and bigger. Greener and greener.

"Yuh?"

"I am not immune to ichthyosaurs or iguanodons or Machairoduses or pteranodons or . . . or . . . Atlantosauruses!"

He was almost smiling. Ancient references formed the plurals of those words in the way of the dead languages that had birthed them. That had changed, while somehow "bacteriums" had never entered the saprophytic Terrali language. Then he frowned.

"What's a Mackerodus?"

"Haha, caught you on one! You and all your last-minute cramming with paleontology! Machairodontinae, subfamily Felidae," she said with eidetic glee. "Sabertooth tiger."

"Oh. Yuh, that probably is what the Bah'ram's people created or tried to, bioengineering those feline fetuses they brought out. Well, we'll just have to—ha!"

Two telits had flashed on, clearly indicating emissions. Those two little telltale readouts told the story: evidence of technology on Jauhar!

"They *are* down here!" he shouted, and squeezed her.

"Someone is. With a techno-employment of energy. Way over there to the . . . well, west from here. West. Jim?"

"Yes? What? Yuh? Look at that! Those are trees, Cicada! That's a coniferalis, sort of a pre-pine— and it's scraping the sky! See the giant ferns. Lots and lots of rain down here!"

"Jim. Let's keep going straight down. Or nearly,

to the temperate zone. Let's just save the source of
the emissions for later, I mean. All right?"

Her calm voice made him feel as if it had rained
on his birthday—which still happened on Earth,
depending upon what climatic conditions happened to be scheduled on the anniversary of one's
birth. The thought flashed that surely on Joharah
it rained on everyone's birthday; judging from the
size of those ferns, it must rain every day. He
bounced right back on the trampoline of his own
uncheckable elation.

"Yes!" His voice was still loud and high, and he
couldn't be bothered trying to grab onto it and
haul it down. "Yes, I understand. First Jim and
Cicada sample Jauhar as people; *then* Lurie and
Allayth lift and stub-wing it over to visit . . .
whatever and whoever is the source of the emissions. New Baghdad, maybe."

" 'New Meccah,' more like."

"Very good!" He squeezed her again, without
willing it. Silly. He just couldn't help it. Down
and down. "I'll bet you're right, too. All right. We
key for soonest planetfall well above the equator,
on optimum terrain. Or rather jauharain. Prefera-
bly surrounded by trees—hm. Hard to avoid
that!"

"And with a stream nearby."

"Sensors primed for H2O concentration, prefer-
ably running, though I think that part will be up to
us to confirm visually."

Down, and down, and down. They saw a
pterosaur—which did not like their size or appearance, and scatted—and then pterosaurs and
an excited Jimajin Allayth thought of the gigantic
bird that had anciently been a part of the literature
of his original people. *Rukh*. That had been trans-

lated as "roc," just as one *jinni* and its plural *jann*
had become "genie" and "genies," when the
sensual-unto-salacious *The Tale of a Thousand
Nights and a Night* became the kiddybook *The
Arabian Nights.*

Call me Wazir, he thought briefly and grandly,
not *Vizier!*

They saw trees and trees and trees, most con-
sisting of masses of foliage forming canopies at
the tips of long, long straight boles. Lepidodendroids; conifers; giant ferns; ginkgoids, and . . .
weirdies, Allayth mused, noting some twisty configurations that might have been designed during
nightmares. Calamites from the carboniferous,
thirty meters tall and more. Great gymnosperms
from the Jurassic and coniferales from every era,
on Earth. All were mixed into this planet's
Paleo-meso-cenozoic brew—or more aptly,
well-heated stew. Spicing the pot, he mused, was
Pterodactylus spectabilis, which he had just seen.
And other giant saurians, he assumed, with, presumably . . . sabertooth tigers?! Impossible! A
madman's dream. A wealthy, brilliant madman's
dream, he corrected mentally.

And . . . people? Breechclouted spear-
bearers?

He expected to see none, not down there.
Civilized people, "native" for hundreds of years
and all dark-haired and tending to big noses,
would be over there to the west in whatever installation they had set up, to live and observe (and
tinker and tamper?). He smiled, running a finger
down his own sizable nose. Nuh; none of the
fun-but-ridiculous old stuff of the movies of the
twentieth and twenty-first centuries (with their
nostalgiludicrous renascence in the twenty-

sixth). Edgar Burroughs and the movies gave, and
Science took away. No Carson Napier on
Venus—not at its pre-saganation temperatures
above 400° and not in its present high-tech set-
tlements, either, cursing that awful rotation. None
of that ancient movie "Planet of the Dinosaurs" in
which the crew of spaceship *Odyssey* battled
Brontosaurus and T. Rex and mighty Allosaurus
and one crewmember was skewered on the big
forehorn of a triceratops—which Allayth assumed had been a peaceful herbivore with all it
could do just to feed that big body. (The six-
metric-ton bull elephant of old Africa had to eat
and eat 18 hours of every 24, just to take in the
necessary 140-280 kilos of fodder necessary to
keep it alive and in shape to feed tomorrow. Allayth felt safe in assuming that Jauharan dinosauria would be very busy just eating—and
dodging the carnivores among them, notably T.
Rex.) No. No world at the planetary core for David
Innes or the redoubtable Tarzan to visit. No Duare,
or Dian the Beautiful, or other Burroughs bitch-
heroines spurning dopey Victorian males.

*Science tooketh away. No Terrible Lizards with
jiggly cantilevered Raquel Somebody or Pamela
Bottaro to chase. The movies and Burroughs
gaveth and Science tooketh away.*

And Science, in the person of man called The
Bah'ram, surely dead a milennium, had given it
all back!

*And . . . Allahumma; King Lizard may well
pound thunderously around down there on two
clawed feet with his ridiculous "hands" and jaws
far from ridiculous in that meter-long skull; 45 to
50 metric tons of* Tyrannosaurus Rex. *And down
and down* Cygnet *fell.*

They saw no T. Rex. No allosaurs. They saw more pterodactyls, and no birds—none whatever.

"Haven't been invented yet," Allayth said, practically dancing up and down. Allayth up: Cygnet down.

That could not have been a glimpse of old Three-horn the ridiculously armored herbivore, could it? Surely not. And yet—Down and down. Science giveth back! She saw a frilled lizard big as a horse and he missed it. They did not see the little band of sixteen in breechclouts, with spears, four of them in chains. They saw Jauhar al-Ajr but not Johara. They saw forest but not trees.

Down and down. They spotted the clearing from two kilometers up and several distant. A stream trickled, not far. They swooped, whooping, trembling with excitement and grateful that Cygnet knew what it was doing when they did not. They settled, down and down amid trees that made the ship far less significant and people mere tiny irrelevancies. Down and down, and dear God that was a towering fungoid excrescence taller than a man; enough mushroom there to garnish an army's worth of steaks!

Bump, and bump, and shudder-thump. Down. Planetfall.

It was the Eden of the ancient legends. With serpents, oh yes with snakes. Without apples. Without, they assumed, a benignly watching, terribly parentally punishing, interfering god or God.

(They did not know then about King Dragon, Messenger of Allah and His servant be he blessed and live eternal, the Bah'ram.)

Had Cicada only been properly prim and sensible, Allayth would not have had to be. As she was

excited and anxious to race right out onto Jauhar
into Eden, he was forced into the other role. She
went Child-sensation; he had to become Parent-
practical.

Boots. "*Jim*—it is thirty-five *degrees* out there.
It's *warm*. And *hu*-mid!"

Boots. And gloves. Sleeves, long sleeves into
the gauntlets. (Same argument. Same parent.
Stolid, practical . . . Jimajin Allayth!)

He had found what might be a weapon and
what could be a real menace to so heavily forested
a planet. Precisely why the one-piece paracadmium fire ax was aboard neither was sure. It was.
He mandated that one of them must carry it while
the other bore the repair laser.

"That ax is *heavy!*"

"All right then, I'll carry the ax."

"Jim—Jimajin! The beamer's even *heavier!*"

He got his way—though he really wanted none
of the clothing and weight of the tools/potential
weapons. Never mind whether he agreed with
himself or not. Somewhere within the newish
child-sensation role she had slid into, she agreed.
He got his way, though he had to be a villain to
accomplish it. Maybe that was all she wanted, he
mused, tugging on the gauntlet and taking the
long heavy laser repair device. It was designed for
use in space. Wonderful. In space it would have
been light. Just unwieldy . . .

They went forth into Eden, and they walked,
and now and again skipped, and by and by the ax
was stood ("right here, so we'll know just where it
is, all shiny and sensible") and the beamer, as the
repair Thing was called, was far too heavy to be
lugged on and on, and so it had to be set
aside (propped up for visibility and swift and easy

snatching if necessary) frightful noises came out
of the forest, animal noises, and now and again a
really hideous screechy scraawk jagged down
from the sky like a lightning bolt of sound, and in
order to *feel* these leaves, this lovely lacy ferny
stuff, one glove—just one, mind—*had* to come off,
and it was all warm and nicely humid and the air
felt wonderful and even smelled good and oh that
sky!—and soon they were disporting themselves,
in Eden.

They danced. They squealed out remarks and
pure wordless happiness. They ran and she rolled
and he fell, which provided his opportunity for
rolling amid odd grass or pre-grass, antegrass,
and ferns and ferns and ferns. The sky! Was there
ever such a sky! Such an azure, a pale cerulean, a
blue moss agate; such wispy clouds of purest
new-milled cottonil and gilded ancient's-beard?
Never! Never on Earth for centuries and centuries!
And never never never such fungi! Basidomycetes Rex!

"Beautiful!" Cicada cried, falling to her knees
(already green-stained) to embrace a magenta
mushroom that just topped her, when she knelt.
And it was barely in the shade, at the edge of the
sunlight!

"Deadly, deadly poison," he called, staring up
the straight bole of a pre-pine, antepine, an
enormously thick javelin lofting straight up a
hundred meters and more. "Morel, Cicada. Dead-
liest nightshade."

"Die young!" she called. "There's no night on
Jauhar!"

"Lots of shade, though."

"Oh yes, lots of shade. A million trees. A billion
trees! There were giants on the planet in those

days, and they were trees, trees! Stalwart, straight, sentry trees! Cerulean and azure sky—even turquoise! See? Over there, near—look there! That cloud looks like a gilt-edged snowbank. White! So white, these clouds! Painted, gilded, tinged with the gold of Jauhar's happy hot sun.''

"Hot is right," he said, not-looking at a mighty disk that could not be blotted even by an uplifted hand. Jauhar hugged mother sun like a nervous child; huge and full of warmth, that sun. (It was a bit larger than Sol, and about the same termperature, and Jauhar slightly farther out from its sun. So what? Let such practical scientific nonsense be wrapped up neatly in a piece of paper and wetted, and thrown far. Who needed pesky facts, in Eden?)

She threw a glove at him. He threw a glove at her. So much for those damned practical hot gauntlets. They were immune to practically everything, and native bacteria had been et up hundreds of ears ago.

They drew in the aromas and odors of fungi and lichen, manifold and multiform. They revelled in the sounds of a billion billion insects and now and again they were silent at the beast-cry that sirened or bellowed from the forest. The forest! Cones, hanging and falling, littering the terrain (jauharain!). Green smells. A clump of snowy showy mushrooms the tallest of which was three or four meters atop a stalk she could have hidden behind: the shortest was knee-high and fat, a white white parasol nigh two meters in diameter. A fat elf in a white sun-hat, he said, and they laughed and laughed.

They fell silent at sight of watchers, long-tailed apes that were not apes, and it was impossible not

to think about humans and pre-humans. Shy
when they knew they were seen, the trio fled into
the jungle, in an eerie silence. And in that forest of
gigantic ferns and conifers and twisty shapes and
lichen that crept and crawled and crawled and
spired and spread and lofted and dangled, too,
like that Spanish "Moss' which was not moss . . .

Noises. *Sinister* noises. Bellows and hoots,
Maynard Ferguson and the final scene of *Don
Giovanni;* elephantine sounds and the manic
jangle of Conan al-Sayth and his Mezzozoic
Syntheviola. Beasts, both placental and sauroid.
Giant feet stomping. Great dagger-lined snouts
lifted to open and pour forth sound.

Not possible. Not possible, any of it. And present, all here present: Science giveth back. Ever-
visible flora; ever audible fauna.

Allayth pounced before her in a long leap with
more height than grace. "I *do* feel lighter in
point-nine-two gravity!" (He alit staggering.)

"Hail!" Lurie cried smiling. "Iyam John Carter, finest swordsman on two worlds with kilometer-long leaps. Wanna fight?" She drew a mock sword with a "wheep" sound and managed not to giggle.

"What's that make me, Dejah Tordos?"

"Thoris, Thoris, didn't you ever read? But of course! She'd have had a chest more outy than yours—but not bilobate like mine—and a double lot of belly and bottom, and no navel at all, egg-laying Dejah Thoris! But—it should be Carson of Venus, shouldn't it!"

"Yes! Carson Napier!" He made a sweeping bow: Carson of Jauhar.

"Right, right!" She made a dramatic arms-wide gesture. "Ah my prince—take me! Let only the planet be virgin!"

They did that. Clothes all over the ground, the meso-cenozoic ground. Constant sounds of fauna; constant sight of flora. The big nearest moon went over. Fast.

"You know," she said, lying on her back on the planet and squinting at its blue, blue sky dominated by sun, "those absolutely ghastly sounds off in the woods, or the jungle or whatever's the word . . . you know what we were carefully not provided with, Adhem? Arms. Armaments! Weapons of any sort."

"We have the beamer—"

"Hardly a particle beamer, though!"

"—and an ax that wouldn't break on a chunk of granite. I think the beamer would do for even a T. Rex."

"Makeshift, Jim darling. Our ingenuity. I mean real weapons. They carefully gave us none."

"True. I never even thought to mention."

"I did."

"Are you a CSP agent, Cicada?"

"How can I be? I am mate in Eden to Adhem—I am Eve!"

"Abu ben Adhem."

"A ridiculous phrase: 'Father Son of Adam!' "

"Ah, pragmatist! You—"

"Pragmatist!" she echoed. "Lying naked on my back beside a man on a planet that is the model for Eden?— under the bluest sky in the universe? No no, that's like the birds, pragmatism is. It hasn't been invented yet!"

"Try this. We have no armaments for the same reason that Margaret Mead and R.F. Burton—"

"Barton."

"—took tape recorders and pen and paper only to those islands back in the pre-Transition Era, and not guns!"

"Yes," she said softly, and he knew her mind had wandered into a new meadow. It was a pretty place: "Jimajin! This is The Beginning! The *in principiam* of every religious cultus. Weapons would be obscene! This is . . . idyllic!"

"Except for the insects." He'd learned; if he kept his statements short, she couldn't interrupt. Back on Earth he wouldn't have tolerated her penchant for interruption.

"Pragmatist!" She punched him. "Obscene realist! So there are insects and we can feel them bite. We can't be infected; with our bioengineered *corpuses*, they won't even raise welts."

"I feel them."

"I want to sleep out here!"

He went pragmatic when she said that. In the father role, he said lots of pragmatic, practical, sensible things. And they slept out under the

blue, blue sky of the planet called Jewel of
Heaven.

That was lovely. Waking up was strange. The
serpent was no trouble, really; only a scare. Far
less interested in them than they were in it and
afflicted with shyness besides, it headed back into
the woods at good speed. No problem. The problem stemmed from this planet's rotation.

They had arrived in daylight, the sun taking up
lots and lots of the sky, and had spent hours and
hours in daylight. They ate, revelled, dictated,
played, talked, played, and went to sleep in daylight. (That had been easy, after so much exertion
and breathing so much fresh air and then the
exertion of sex.) And they awoke with half the sun
still visible, which was still more in the sky than
at any time on Earth. And the nearest moon was
going over. Again.

Waking up with eyelids closed but seeing
bright yellow-white was *wrong*. "Weird," Allayth said, and received agreement. "At least it's
coming on for sunset."

"And will be for the next . . . what? Four or
five hours? And then it will be night for fifty hours
plus? And my, ah, lower stomach is making funny
noises. That snake that just scared me into pre-
fibrillation isn't the serpent in Eden, Jim. The
rotation is. The damned rotation. I think I'll just
not stay, thanks."

Half smiling, he glanced over at the ship. How
tiny it looked! Almost fragile, all shining and
compact, surrounded by so many tall, tall trees.

A few minutes later the real serpent invaded
Eden, on two legs. It was not a reptile at all, and it
was four meters tall.

9

Year 83: Today, after the insane and ungrateful attempt by the self-styled Sons of Mahomet on the Comm-quarters, He spoke to us all. Al-Bah'ram himself! How strong his voice, emanating from every speaker in the world—that is, on the station. How we should love to *see* Him! Yet all understand his position and the necessity for his remaining apart from us; above us. It is enough to hear him. How commanding, how inspiring that voice and his words! He is eternal. He watches over us and keeps us. Glory to Allah and His al-Bah'ram!

—journal of 796 Muhammad,
Station Bah'ram

The bear emerged from the forest just on the other side of *Cygnet* and its roar was enough to stir ferns fifteen meters away.

Between ship and humans lay the shining thigh-sized cylinder and snout of the beamer, all bright and inviting and deadly even to impossibly overgrown ursinoids. They stared at each other, humans and monster. It had to look down and down. Someone said *"Allahuma—my God!"* Again the ursine titan bellowed forth a growl and again the feathery leaves of ferns trembled, meters and meters away.

"The beamer!" That was Cicada, and she started running.

"No!" That was Allayth, and he whirled. The shining ax was nearby and he snatched it up. He had only just got his boots on.

With another snarl that went trailing off into a rumble, the bear started forward, walking erect. Its eyes were fixed on the little human running toward him. Its thigh, just above the knee, banged the jumpship. That surely would not have happened had the beast not had its attention on the racing woman less than half its height and a fourth its weight. It bumped *Cygnet*, and its snarl was of annoyance, not pain.

Jim Allayth saw it and never never forgot: with no more than that snarl and a sideward glance of annoyance unto anger, the bear *slapped* the jumpship.

Allayth did not see the bear register pain, or the hull dent. He did see *Cygnet* slowly, slowly tilt, as if leaning away from the blow. He screamed something at the top of his lungs; no one ever knew what. He saw the ship fall. slowly, half-pivoting as if trying to twist itself away. Toppling metal flashed beautifully refulgent in the otherworld sunlight. The noise was thunderous and Allayth felt impact in feet and legs. The mingled screech of metal was the sound of a million fingernails across a million chalkboards.

Cygnet had become a casualty while Cicada, clothing fluttering and hair blowing behind her in trailing ribbons, ran for the repair Thing. Toward the ursine Thing. It, after another annoyed and only mildly interested glance at *Cygnet*, advanced. That lumbering step covered close to two meters.

The bear advanced another heavily thudding pace and Allayth was sure he felt that, too. It towered above fallen ship and running woman. A ghastly hirsute model for the Colossus of Rhodes. More than twice *Cicada's* height and several times her bulk and mass, and seeming bigger still in that shaggy coat. (It did *not* belong in this climate, Allayth thought; it did not belong in this planet's lower temperate zone—it did not belong on this planet!) And she ran, insane or brave or fixated past cerebration on the beamer and Allayth hefted the ax, knowing horror for fallen *Cygnet* and fear for Cicada. Despair lurked but stood back while adrenaline pumped.

Cicada Lurie reached the repair laser and practically skidded to a stop.

She bent for the beamer. She laid hands on it. The bear moved, bending. Allayth yelled and hurt his throat with the frantic scream.

Lurie picked up the beamer. Madly, completely without thought, Allayth swung the ax back over his shoulder. Cicada started to level the repair device. The bear's racing-swinging paw, claws long as Cicada's hands, swung.

Cicada clung to the beamer all the way, while she flew seven or eight meters. Trailing a wake of scarlet dots and making not a sound, she was stopped by a fat vine-draped tree that shook violently with the impact.

She struck it three or so meters above the ground, crosswise and hard enough to make a noise loud as an ax-fall. Twigs fell from the tree and a bright orange bromeliad floated down in unconcerned loveliness. The beamer went flying into the forest and banged off another tree. Cicada wrapped halfway around the bole of the tree her spine had struck, seemed to hesitate, suspended there, and slowly slid down. She dropped to the ground and most definitely did not move. A couple of twigs landed on her and the flower fluttered to the ground nearby.

Allayth had yelled something—no one ever knew what—when the beast slapped her, and he had hurled the ax. The act was irrational, of course, but rationality was a protoplasmic thing that had nothing to do with bears big as jump-ships. It fled him when he saw Cicada struck with force more than sufficient to topple a jumpship.

The ax flashed and twinkled beautifully and struck the immense ursinoid to rebound in an end-over-ending flash-flash-flash of silvery paracadmium, bent. The bear did not growl or snarl this time. It roared. And it came for Allayth. There was exactly one thing Jim Allayth could do.

Cygnet lay broken, and unimportant.

Cicada lay broken and unmoving.

Allayth ran. The bear followed in short body-swinging strides that were long because of its height. A beast from time's dawn pursued a weaponless man, and the man was by far the less. What might have been petrific fear instead galvanized. Allayth ran, fueled by adrenaline. Technology lay broken and panic and savagery fled into the Meso-Cenozoic forest.

Trees and bushes seemed to attack him. He ran in forest; rain forest, not jungle. Underfoot was a detritus at once crackly and squelchy, dead and

dry and mulch-damp; wet and new-life suppor-
tive. All around flourished ferny plants and fungi
and lichen; all around rose gigantic straight-boled
trees. He ran, and the bear followed. A snarl
speeded the quarry. A bellowing growl made
twigs and leaves quiver all around him. He ran.
And ran. Light diminished in the woods, under
the canopy of green. He heard the crashing behind
him. He did not look back; he knew it came and
came and he knew that to look back was to slow a
bit, was stupid, was probably to guarantee death.
He had that much presence of mind, and he was
proud of it in that small section of his mind that
was functioning beyond the primitive.

Behind him limbs broke and crashed as they
were hurled aside by arms with dagger-like claws.
Even in the noise of his own passage through the
forest Allayth could hear the stomp of huge
clawed feet. He ran, fell, rolled, was hurt, scrambled up running, ran, struck a tree and caromed,
staggering, hurting, was kept from falling by impact with another tree, heard the bear coming,
coming; ran, felt his leg raked and his pants leg
caught, yanked desperately at the snag and tore
free to stagger into a tree, pawed his way around it
and fought free of a curtain of helical vines like
Celtic knotwork. Ran, tripped over the base of
those vines, which swung from the tree they
clung to eight or nine meters above. He staggered,
tore shirt and pants and pants and skin, took a
hard rap on the ankle that might have crippled but
for the boot and his desperation, threw himself to
his feet, running before he was fully vertical,
staggered, ducked a dying branch that raked his
back, ran, ran, ran.

His heart pounded and he heard his breathing shot with sobs. He smelled nothing and saw only barriers and he heard the bear, coming, coming. He ran. The cylinder that was his calculator-computerlink went with his shirt pocket and a line of epidermis off his chest. Heart surged and adrenaline spurted and he ran.

The mass of cones and runners, vines and fallen twigs and branches sought constantly to hold and trip him and he staggered. Had he not been pursued he'd never have made it. Too often his boot sole slipped on fungi. His very desperation maintained the precipitate flight over terrain that was an impossible obstacle course.

A floral canopy blotted the blue blue sky in the forest's own twilight. His lungs hurt and he knew that he was breathing only because he heard the panting. When a briar bit his hand he briefly remembered how he and Cicada and thrown their gauntlets at each other. *Cicada!* Sweat drenched him and ran so that he had to wipe his face with a dirty hand to clear his eyes of his own salt water. He groaned when some impossible twisting formation of Jauharan flora twisted his arm and tore away his combination chronograph-calculator-translator.

He ran, staggered, fell to a knee that painfully impacted an erupting vine-base thick as his wrist and almost immediately stepped across a green and tan and brown snake just as thick. It was fleeing, too—from him. It fled him and he fled the bear. The bear came and came, crashing.

It will give up, Allayth told himself, and ran. *It has to!*

The bear kept coming.

He floundered through an entanglement of whippy brush and incredibly stout vines no thicker than styluses—and aerial roots that formed it all into a great green mound. Through them, and he burst directly into what that thick rich growth partially disguised: the small territory surrounding a den of dog-wolves or wolf-dogs. Hyaenodons.

The ground seemed to erupt furry canine shapes and snarling fangs in a living volcanic mass. It barked and snarled in surprise and anger and some fear. He heard yelps, too, and the yips of the young. Newly fearful and half blind he crossed that clearing without seeing anything but shapes and teeth. He plunged into another warren of twisted air-root bushes and the curling twisting killing vines that used them. He had not slowed, had not more than brushed one furry animal a bit smaller than a black-and-tan coonhound. Vines and viney bushes seemed to attack him, fight his intrusion into their maze of a territory. He floundered on, being struck, raked, tripped, torn. All by flora, not the noisy fauna behind him.

There was a lot more noise behind him, now.

The bear burst through, still following, and the noise was a mad cacophony that approached the deafening. Allayth fell, wallowed, flailing and kicking at vines and twisting whippy branches, whining, gasping for every breath. The bear had accidentally invaded the territory of others. Younglings were present, and the hyaenodons defended, males and females alike. The noise level rose until he could not hear his panting and his curses.

He wallowed out of that tangled maze amid a

crackle of dead sticks, stems that had died after growing overtall and bending to root with their own tips and start anew.

He raced up along the huge, twisting pathway formed by a fallen tree. It would have been too precarious had he not been fleeing. He had no time to consider its width, its elevation, or let his equilibrium take pause. Pursued, he was capable of breaking records for speed and endurance, balance and jumping; records he would never have approached without the pursuit of death, even if he had trained. (*Cicada!*) Pursuit proved a more effective stimulus than any steroids or drugs.

The pursuit continued, amid horrid noise; the bear forged on. Now it was wading through a score of barking leaping snarling snapping clinging chewing dog-wolves.

"Man's best friend," Jim Allayth sobbed, for he could talk no other way and was stupid enough to try.

Then he was trapped. The elevation of the fallen tree under his feet had risen and risen, and now directly ahead was a vertical one two meters in diameter and seemingly of infinite, unbranched height. To his right a long hill fell away, crowded with thorny creepers bearing lovely pallid flowers and arthritically twisted bushes sprouting thorns long as his fingers. Bear and hyænodons had burst forth on his left. He could never succeed in running back past them. He turned to try anyhow, or to fall into the thorns. And saw and heard, in a raucous guttural profusion of sound that blotted all other sound and interfered with thought, a battle. Not a running fight or even a fight, but a battle.

The canine pack might have attacked the bear, had he not invaded their den area, and they might not. They had, and the bear fought, and they did not give it up.

It went on and on, amid snarls and barkings, growls and thundering roars, shrill yips and cries of pain. Blood and saliva flew and spattered the combatants. A score of pre-dawn pre-wolves and the gigantic grandfather of all beardom. The bear's coat was matted with saliva and blood that glistened darkly. Hyænodons leaped to cling with their jaws or fell to snap and leap again. Hyænodons were hurled screaming to slam into ground and trees, to lie moaning and broken or to return despite limps and obvious pain. The bright dark sheen of blood coated the bear's coat in a half-score places, oozed in a dozen more.

Ragged and panting, Allayth could only watch. Blood oozed or trickled from his many scratches. Sweat washed it down, stinging. He was even more conscious of the heat, now that he no longer stirred air by running.

Hyænodons would not give up. They died and were wounded. The towering ursinoid did not die, but it was wounded and rage gave way to fear that approached desperation. It retreated. It backed, stomping and flailing, snarling and roaring and whining, and the leaping circling snapping pack kept at it.

The battle left Allayth, tore into the forest.

He quitted his tree, fearful and in danger of losing his balance now that he noticed and was able to think about it. Back on the ground, he twisted and tore and broke off a chunk of still-living tree. He had no gun or beamer or ax or

chronograph or computerlink. He had a club. And he heard a rumbly growl, low and throatily deep. He turned.

At the edge of a broken thicket four slavering low-slung beasts had come back or paused to glare at him. Their ears were back. The hair behind their heads was up and spiky. Their snouts hideously furled. Tool-user and Best Friend faced each other in primeval wood.

"Nuh," Allayth said quietly, "you don't want me. I'm no competitor or menace either, and stringy eating. I'm Man. You may not know it, but your goal and destiny is to be man's best friend."

Strangely, noses unwrinkled and three of four pair of ears cocked as he spoke. One beast made a whining noise. Then another turned to go after the pack and the bear, and the others wheeled to join it.

"Man's best friend," Allayth muttered weakly, and fell down as adrenaline went wherever adrenaline goes when it is no longer needed. His heartbeat sought normalcy.

He lay there a long while, recovering. Shedding sweat and blood and letting heartbeat and breathing move back toward their proper levels. Trying to think, and trying not to think. The ship—was it dead? Cicada . . . he squeezed his eyes shut and gulped. *Cicada!* She could not be alive. She was broken into a limp thing. Shreds of bone must have punctured her skin, organs, and clothing.

At last he rose. A multiply scratched and contused man in shredded clothing—and fine equhyde boots, courtesy the Directorate of a distant planet called Earth. It was far, far more distant than it had been an hour or two ago.

He spent the next four days—just under a day, on Jauhar al-Ajr, where a complete day and night contained 128 hours—searching for the ship, for Cicada, for his own trail back through the forest. He found none of them, ever.

10

Year 93: I have been listening to my mother's
diary, though this is not Authorized Activity.
How strange the life of a woman! How weird
that when this mission began women actually
supposed themselves equal; how majestic of
Allah and al-Bah'ram not to destroy them for
their temerity! How fortunate I am to be a
man!

—814 Sareed, on his 15th birthday

Soon after sunset, rain fell. Allayth behaved
stupidly again; he tried to continue searching for
his own trail. Had he not been thoroughly lost
already, the rain took care of it. Only when he was
soaked did he take shelter under a ridiculously
large upgrowth of discomycetic fungus, yellow
and white and a fulvous hue. He waited and
waited. Now and again he shivered a little, as rain
and lack of sunlight lowered the temperature
even within the heat-preserving haven under the
forest canopy. Naturally the miseries came on,
and he wallowed in depression and self-
castigation.

He had boots, a few rags of clothing, and a club.
A club! Somewhere, with a piece of his shirt, lay
the fat pencil-shape that was his link with Cyg-

net's computer. I should have stopped and picked
it up. (Sure. And been slain by that grandfather of
all bears.) Somewhere, with a piece or two of skin,
lay his wristpiece: chronograph, 96,000-entry
translator, calculator. He should have paused to
retrieve it. (*Sure, and been overhauled and taken
apart by that ursinodon. Or just hurled, like
Cicada, to break.*

(*Cicada!*) Cicada. He knew she had to be dead.
She had been hurled several times the length of
her own body, thrown like the rag doll of a bitter
child. It was her spine that had struck the big
tree's trunk, and she had wrapped halfway
around it, backward. Vertebrae popping, sever-
ing, slicing through nerves. Ribs splintering, jab-
bing through her chest, her heart . . . he shuddered, made a sobbing sound, and hurled that
thought from his brain.

*She was young and happy and then she became
a figure of real tragedy and then she was dead.* So
Cicada Lurie had said of Cicada of the old Philippines. And then she was dead.

What could he have done? He had thrown the
ax—which was reflex, about as intelligent as letting himself be persuaded to sleep outside the
ship. (Conveniently, ingeniously, he was able to
blame himself for that. Never mind that it had
been at her insistence.

(*I should have been firm,* he reflected, flogging
himself as by now billions of his kind had done.)

And somewhere lay jumpship *Cygnet.*

Was it dead? Broken, like Cicada?

Did it matter? Surely it was no longer capable of
lifting him off this horrid Eden-seeming Hell of a
planet.

Let's sleep out, she had said. (Ever-visible flora

and ever-audible fauna became a grey curtain and
a hiss of rain that drowned all other sight and
sound.)

*Yes . . . I may be sleeping out now for a long,
long time. If I live.*

Rain fell and fell. In the dark, without thunder
or electricity, without wind. Rain fell straight
down, paler than the dark, a ghost-curtain on a
demon planet. One miserable man from Earth
made himself as small as possible under the yel-
lowish dome of a fungus-thing whose thigh-thick
stem was a meter and a half tall and whose
umbrella—apt description, just now!—was as
broad. Mister five by five.

On Earth, rain had been bringing, accompany-
ing, symbolizing the miseries for millennia. On
Jauhar? For a millennium, perhaps? Less?

Maybe natives or rather "natives" loved it, for it
doubled the coolth after the setting of a sun that
filled a quarter of the sky and reigned hot over the
land for 72 hours at a stretch. That only made him
reflect miserably that this darkness would prevail
for 56 hours. More than two days, Earth time. Two
"days" and three periods of sleep worth of darkness. Or worse, three "days" and two sleeps.

*We slept just before sunset. Clever of us. Even
that was wrong, one more piece of sheerest
stupidity. To awake in darkness, to have to spend
the equivalent of a day in darkness! I Should
Have Known . . .*

Thus he wallowed, and it rained, grey and hissing.

They did not use her after the rain, either. The
one captive still eyed her hungrily. The leader of
their captors noticed, and saw that they were not

near each other. Joharah was glad. She huddled in the hissing darkrain and, trying not to feel miserable, tried to watch the progress of a whiskery twinerbitch. It would never reach its goal, either.

Sifayah was so badly frightened that she was only just able to stammer out her message. Then the plump fourteen-year-old collapsed shuddering and sobbing. Her mother held her and rocked her as if she were still a child. Her mother was at once proud and sorry for her.

Sifayah had done nothing she had not done before. Just after the darkrain, with her hair tucked and bundled up, she went for a walk in the velvety fog that eddied along the bank of the river which Kwait called its own. Her thoughts were on Joharah, who was her cousin. Sifayah liked the soft wet coolth of the fog and always had, and the way her ankles disappeared into the grey-white ground-cloud that left them wet and glistening. She paused to sit just at the water's edge, thinking, enjoying the night and the process of being alone to think.

It was a nightfall like other nightfalls; a darkrain like other darkrains, and a fog like other such fogs.

But this time the ground-cloud held the Messenger of Allah and Bah'ram. Not aflight; he was in the water itself. One moment the water was there, dark and undisturbed; the next he was there. Water lizard and girl stared at each other, and one of them shivered in fear. Yet it showed her no teeth, no menace.

"*I am the Messenger of the Living God and the Bah'ram, may his name be blessed,*" King Dragon or a water lizard said, and its eerily soft voice spoke her language perfectly. There was a strange hollow sound about the words, as though they emanated from within a rot-hole in a great broad tree. *"Kwait has not pleased, in allowing a fine young bride to flee alone into the forest. Raafar's appearance has nought to do with his being the finest hunter in Kwait. His sons are needed. Kwait needs them and all the world needs them. Go to him, got to Raafar and lie with him. It is the will of Allah and his Bah'ram! And bid the people of Kwait know that they must again endure the Cooling, for they are far from perfect and yet displease. Go!"*

The terrified girl went. She never looked back. (Later, no one found any sign of King Dragon's presence there. It was true that Sifayah had always been a strange girl.)

Her people were not astonished that *Malik-rukh* knew of their affairs, and took interest. He had done so before. They nodded sadly that they must endure the coming of Zamhar. But that too was normal, and none so terrible. Many secretly believed that they could never achieve The Bah'ram's concept of perfection, and that the Cooling would always come, just as rain always came after sunset and after dawn. Everyone was pleased for Raafar. True, some women shuddered, and more than one maiden was much relieved. Mating with that beautifully formed man with the hideous face was an honor they were happy to cede to Sifayah. She had always been a strange girl, anyhow.

Poor Raafar was already stricken by Joharah's flight from him. Now he took Sifayah's fit of trem-

ors and sobs as fear and horror of him, rather than
of King Dragon—or of hysteria. Malik-rukh was
after all Allah's Messenger and their friend, all
good and deserving of all their love. Raafar
Saurslayer was not capable of conceiving of fear
of King Dragon. Raafar did not seek to lay claim to
Saifayah, or even wait for her to recover. Allah
and Bah'ram, after all, had not come to him to
command *him* to lie with her.

What could the Leader of Kwait say? He was not
even sure he believed Sifayah, who had ever been
a strange girl. "I go for my woman," Raafar told
him, his mouth having to twist hideously to form
the words. He said nothing more, but took
weapons and his extravagant new cloak and once
again departed Kwait; the best hunter and tracker
anyone knew set off after Joharah.

It had seemed hours and hours in the darkness
just after sunset, and once it stopped Allayth
wondered how long it had rained. Now it was
growing decidedly chilly. He wished for more
clothing. He wished he had his chronograph.

*Stupid. Who needs a timetelit, trapped on a
planet with 128-hour rotation?* (His stomach
rumbled and his bowels cramped. Already his
body knew that things here were not normal, and
it complained.)

*We are wedded to them, that's why. Time on
our wrists. I would know how long it rained, that's
why. How long it's been . . .*

Cicada . . .

A long, long while later he rose, stretched,
cursed mildly, squinted about. (An hour later?
Ten minutes? What was time? Time was a thing
one wore on one's wrist.)

The world was full of noises, and all were fearful and menacing. A million creatures commented on the rain's end, and all were hungry.
That damned little vine with its almost-leaves like
a merman's whiskers—even it seemed to have
moved close since he had sat. He kicked it,
glanced up at his shelter. God and Stars, the thing
was bright yellow now, on a stem taller than he. A
poison cup ringed the stem, large as his pelvic
girdle. Enough poison there to kill six or seven
giant ursinoids—or a whole pack of hyænodons.

*Wish I had one here now, as company. Man's
best friend. How long before they are, on Jauhar?
Do I have to start it? How does one tame a wild dog
that is not quite a dog?* Had it been instinct that
guided them to heed him, and leave him—or had
they merely been more interested in joining the
pack in the harrying of a beast on the run?

He became aware of light, and looked up. Visible beyond the leaves: a moon. The nearest. Fat up
there, smugly spaceborne. Bigger than a silver
eyeball afloat in Heaven—above Hell!—looking
down on horror and fear and depression.

In a short time he was aware that it had moved.
One could stare at it and never see its movement,
yet know that it had moved. It circled Jauhar
swiftly, that close-in moon that was larger than
Luna. Like the minute hand on a primitive watch.

I wish I had my chronograph.

He went looking for it, slogging, wet, chilly. He
learned the meaning of a very ancient term:
charley-horse. He had two.

He ate nothing, but drank well, of new-fallen
water waiting for the sun to come along and suck
it up. Insects ate; they ate on him. He slogged for
hours. Then, hungry and chilly, he slept.

Climbing onto the basin-shaped mushroom broad as he was tall had been brilliant, except for the ten centimeters of water standing in the cup. Climbing down, he fell. A snake slithered away, at speed. It had good reason, Allayth discovered. The lizard was a third of a meter high at the "Shoulder" and about two long, including the tail, and its tongue seemed about ten kilometers long.

The tongue touched his bare arm and he reacted with a lurch and a cry. Startled, the lizard scuttled away. So did Allayth, with pounding heart and in the opposite direction. (Later he reflected that he might have been three steps from the clearing in which lay *Cygnet*, the ax, Cicada. The lizard might have scurried right across the ax.) (*And then again, I might not have been even close.*)

Tired, very cleverly he went up a helically wrapped rope of vine and over onto a beige (he thought; it was dark) mushroom ten or so meters above the ground. Some sort of flower, a bromeliad or a lichen —who knew in the dark— grew on the parasol, which was firm as flesh-clad bone and perhaps three meters across. He slept there, hungry.

It was still dark when he awoke, cold. A glance in the direction of all the racket showed him the silhouette of an enormous head on an Allayth-thick neck. Remembering that he was a decimeter or so above the ground and looking slightly up at that reptilian head on its serpentine neck, he lay very still and tried not to breathe. He feared the beast heard the rumble of his stomach.

The thing went on, crashing.

Yes. There are dinosauria on Jauhar al-Ajr.

Giant bears, pre-dogs, long-tailed apes-almost-men, giant fungi, pre-pines, pterodactyls, and dinosaurs. Insanity! A mad god's evolutionary games.

He rose shivering and went crouching to the edge of his fungoid bed where his foot went right through the edge and he fell onto and through another smaller mushroom and then another and onto a ground softened by rotting fungi that smelled like a vampire's breath. There were also some nasty twigs that would have hurt even if he had not been nearly naked, which he was.

Now belatedly, he decided to sit and wait for daylight before he went stumbling around in this awful forest, but after an hour (or ten minutes or two hours) he couldn't stand the tense inactivity in which every sound was magnified. He took two squishy steps and looked down upon pallid white buttons.

His stomach rumbled.

Mushrooms, Allayth mused. Sweet, edible snowcap mushrooms. (Unlikely name on Hell! Jauharans would call them something else, and by that other name they would surely be still as sweet.) He squatted. His intestines tried to knot and his stomach rumbled. He broke off one, low to the ground. No collar; no poison cup. Sweet, edible—No! He hurled it from him as he jacked himself swiftly upright on long legs. *No! I know nothing about fungi on this devil-spawned planet!*

Whimpering for a computer, food concentrate, a few chemicals, bidding his stomach shut up, he went on. In darkness. Being lost, and working on being more lost. A kilometer from *Cygnet*? Thirty or forty meters from *Cygnet?*

The snake was no smarter than he. It dropped on him, and it was not big enough. Allayth cried out involuntarily, staggered, lurched, grabbed, staggered, fell, rolled, tore from him a serpent three meters long and little thicker than three fingers, and slammed it against a tree. The snake went limp without even a twitch. It dropped dead. Shivering and goosefleshed, Allayth ground his teeth to keep from yelling. He moved well away, then sat down for awhile to let the shakes go away.

An hour later (or half hour, or twenty minutes), he rose and went on. An hour (or . . . or . . .) after that it hit him. *I have been attacked twice. I fled once and killed once. I have coped! Mighty hunter has slain! Good lord, I am surviving as a primitive man.*   Sure. In boots. Hungry. Scared. Miserable. Depressed. *Cicada!* Did you care, really care? Would we have—

He sat down to feel sorry for himself for awhile. He did not quite cry, but he did a lot of sniffling. And fell asleep.

He awoke in chilly darkness, and he was ravenous.

"Good lord," he muttered aloud, watering a tree's base. "I could have eaten that snake! Stupid, stupid—it was my kill, Mighty Hunter Allayth's first kill! I could have ea—"

Raw? He dry-heaved.

The *squee-conk* noise was very loud and terribly close and it came from *above,* though not from the sky. He moved away from it as fast as he could while trying not to make a sound, enwrapped in an invading mist of mortal dread—in the dark. He heard its crashing movements. Dinosaur. Huge. It was going in another direction.

Despite the fact that his experience had taught him of the shyness of most creatures and his ability to escape and elude, he was wedded to sorrowful perturbation and self-pity. Wallowing in those, he went on. The self-pity wanted only a bit of nurturing to grow into real despair.

With his booted foot he kicked and kicked a sapling while he leaned on it, twisting. Eventually he had a viciously pointed spear about the thickness of four close-pressed fingers. It was sharp at the heavy end, too. The trouble was it was also about five meters long, terminating in a spray of ferny leaves. He spent an hour or so tearing and twisting and stomping it in two. Armed, he went on. Making mean faces to bolster his courage. Mighty hunter bore a green, thick sharp stick some two and a half meters long.

The first time he threw it, it turned up and a bit sidewise.

He had a lance, then, not a spear. He spent another half-hour tearing a limb off a pre-tree bush of some sort that had availed itself of an unusual opportunity to grow tall. Of it he made a thumb-thick stave, just over half his height in length. It was so green it was both hard and too sappy to break with anything approaching ease. Carrying the lance in his right hand, he held the stave in the other and swatted branches and bushes with it as he walked. He had not yet admitted that he was lost.

He came face to face with a hunting hyænodon.

It squatted, snarling. Ears back, hackles bristling, snout wrinkled. They stared at each other.

"Hello, Spot. I am Man, mighty hunter. You'd best either heel or git, before I decide you'd be good to eat."

The wolf-dog stood, showing teeth. It neither snarled nor barked, but held to its intimidation display.

"Git!"

It got. Mighty hunter went on, carrying two sticks and a bit more confidence. His stomach growled, knotted, hurt, and made gas. He let it go with gusto.

The nearest of the three moons came around again, and he wished for a computer—or that he had sense enough to know how many hours of darkness had passed. Fifty? Twenty? No, more than thirty, surely. He probably had not eaten in fifty or so hours. Two days.

I should have remained still. I am lost. I am weakening. I may be starving, and I am most certainly in the midst of plenty. I've even lost some blood, to little wounds and hungry insects a lot better able to take care of themselves than I am. Eat that lovely big amanita and die in agony. But what about the center of that flower? That twisty can-of-worms mass of mushrooms snuggling against the base of that huge one? Perfectly edible Honey Agaric, aren't they? Or the huge one; it's handsome, arrowstraight, without a collar. No poison there. Everything on Jauhar must have come from Earth. Dogs from bioengineered *canis* embryos or maybe *lupus* ones. Mushrooms from . . .

He ate. He ate fungus, the great delicacy of

caves and abandoned mines on Earth. He ate mushroom. And felt wonderful. He went on. He did not die, or even get sick. He just began hallucinating.

11

First, the trees began a subtle undulation. He was irritated by that, and even more irritated when they began to dissolve liquescently into quivery kaliedoscopic streams that flowed undulantly in varying psychotropic colors and ever-changing configurations . . . slowly . . . so slowly . . .

Then amusement took him and he began to giggle, to laugh. He walked on, blundering, reeling without knowing it, laughing without knowing at what . . . slowly . . .

Heroically bearded and muscled, his fine amethyst-pommeled sword at his hip, *Tarf* Jimajin al-Bahluwan rode—slowly, slowly—through the forest of his domain. Trees like ancient cathedrals, yet new and spotless, with fungal altars and larger fungi forming majestic mosques. His enormous steed was a pareiasurus, with a few modifications. The beast's saddle blanket was the hide of a particularly large and ferocious sabretooth tiger, personally slain by Great Lord Jimajin the Brave, also called *al-Zaheer*: Foremost by Decree of Allah. His beast's name was Shirzad, which meant Lion-born. But Jimajin al Bahluwan as often called him Tantor, in his spirals of incredible psychotropism of dreams beams streams steams beteams breams boom breast be by

By his side, on her own steed, was the Great Lord Jimajin's loving shapely (101-50-89) mate, who fought fiercely and mycologically at his side and madly loved him above all things. Her name was Locust and she was as often called al-Hacene: the Beautiful. Clad in her beauty and her pride and her well-blooded dagger of finest paracadmium, she bestrode her own mighty anomodont reptile of the Triassic. Its name was Laxshmy. A stupid beast Tarf Jimajin enjoyed riding now and again, hard.

"Ah, Jimajin," Locust said conversationally and slowly . . . slowly, "I love thee above all things!"

"Yes yes, and once we have reached the Keep of Science to the west, my love, I shall give you the very stars. And a brand-new chronograph, too." He laughed aloud.

"I want only you," she of course said, and they rode heroically and mycologically through the domain that was theirs. The trees shifted, slowly . . . slowly, and Jimajin laughed. A Tyrannosaurus Rex saw them and backed away in fear. It was an object of infinite fascination, Jimajin saw, that changed and multiplied in color and complexity even as he watched. He laughed. His steed, whose name was Walrus, turned to look back at its rider.

"Take into account please," Walrus boomed, "that the following explanation is a crude idea, but all that can be communicated between us. No matter what I say, you will think that you understand me better than you actually do."

"True, true," Jimajin said laughing, "and it is true too that things are seldom what they seem! That T. Rex, for instance. It is composed entirely of sealing wax."

"Treacle," Locust suggested, her voice rising at the end in respectful query rather than correction.

Both leaned back on their reins, then, for a jumpship flashed down and landed neatly just ahead. From it descended a couple wearing, like Jimajin and Locust, next to nothing. The male held up a swordlike object that Jimajin could see was a computerlink, as he could see that its wielder was a mere youth.

"Tarf Jimajin al-Bahluwan, Malik-shah!" that youth most respectfully called. "I beg your indulgence and protection for me and my woman, for we would be under the great spreading wing of your protection."

"Why, he's a mere lad," Locust commented, *sotto voce.*

"True," the Great Lord Jim said, "but a sturdy and brave one!" And more loudly, "Who are you, who would lean on me and walk in my shadow?" He had to curb his laughter.

"My name is Flaerti," the lad said humbly. "I crave only to serve you, who are so wise and unexcitable and decisive!"

"Hmmm," Jimajin the Brave muttered, watching the jumpship's evanescent wavering and trying not to laugh. "And your woman?"

"Hmp," Locust commented in that same so-quiet voice, "woman! A mere clingy *girl* I see—my lord."

"My chosen mate is named Cygnet," the lad said, and she stepped slowly . . . slowly from

him to smile, and bow, and rise flashing into the heavens. And the Great Lord Jimajin knew that soon he would ride her, for he comprehended the very nature of ultimate reality, which was *Musse-roun Basidomycetes Fungironi*: mushroom. Wonderful! He could ride *Cygnet* to the Keep of Science over westward, with this boy Flaerti to help him, and be there a lot sooner and with no danger.

Danger? But I . . . I . . . then he . . . he . . . he saw palaces, the mightiest of mosques, stars, seascapes; he saw new mountains and marveled at their silkiness and the complexity of their hues and shoes; he . . . he . . .

He said firmly, "No, Cicada. No, we will not sleep out. That would be stupid. Some creature might come bumbling along and where would we be? No no. We return to *Cygnet*, and I will use the beamer to cut and sharpen a pair of fine swords and daggers out of stanchions we do not need while you guide us westward, right now, to the source of those technology readings we got. Come along now."

"Yes of course darling," she said. "You are right, of course. Oh Jim dearest, you are so decisive and strong! Even the snake feared you!"

"Dream on, and once we have reached the scientific base, Cicada, Locust, I will give you a token: my chronograph with the translator/ vocalculator capability. And the stars!" And he laughed aloud.

"I want only you, Jimajin," she said, and the bear came out of the forest.

It concentrated on her, trying to eat her. It ignored Allayth's attack until it fell, because the ax

had cut through its leg. Then with that same double-crescent battle ax of his forebears, Allayth slew the bear and cut it open and out popped Cicada unharmed, wearing a mycological smile and a hooded red riding cloak, and his chronograph. Savior Allayth laughed aloud and

Blackness and rain came bringing discorporeality and invisibility and the pristine nave of Notre Dame al-Sofia de Bah'ram, and a silvery sweep of his tempered blade sent the horn flying from the nose of a triceratops which, with a shriek dropped to its knees and implored in a walrustic voice. Contemptuously, almost in passing, Jimajin cracked its head open with the steel-bossed bracer on his left arm. Then he tossed his sword into that hand to lop off the silly little forelegs of a Tyrannosaurus Rex, all in a single long fluid movement and stroke. Wheeling then, he waded laughing into the twenty or so beast-men and began chopping and cleaving and hurling them back until the bear came and he . . .

. . . was standing on a psilocybinic ledge in the bright bright sun. He gazed down upon the fearsome battle: a score or so beast-men, valiantly battling the giant bear. Roaring and snarling in the manner of animals, those almost men, antean throids with their stone weapons, attacked the impossibly huge beast that towered over them. The growls and snarls and thunder-challenging roars of the gigantic ursinoid mingled with the snarls and cries—could that be language?—of the shaggy gorilloids with their scintillant jewelry and mica-flashing axes and spears.

On this scene looked down Jimajin, Lord of the Forest, laughing in his breechclout of sabretooth

leopard. At his side hung his fine gem-tipped
sword. Low on his back was slung his psy-
chotropus-hide quiver of fine stout arrows and
in his hand his fine wood-and-horn bow. He
laughed aloud.

Two arrows in the bear's back did not stagger
him or make him turn, and Jimajin's shouts could
not compete with the insane cacophony of animal
noises. Irritated and yet laughing, he tore loose a
chunk of mycological mica from the cliff's edge
(cliff? It swiftly, undulantly metamorphosed into
an enormous lepidodendroid tree). His unerring
throw bounced the jagged stone off the back of the
bear's skull. That gained its attention. Staggered,
the ursinoid turned with a bellowing roar that
stirred Jimajin's hair. Calmly and slowly . . .
slowly with plenty of time, Tarf Jimajin al-
Bahluwan nocked an arrow and sent it straight
into the beast's eye. The left. He laughed aloud
and wondered if the animal was ambinocular.
Deliberately switching bow to right hand and
pulling the arrow with his left, Allayth sighted
. . . the sonic power of that roar of pain rocked
him, and the monster came for him, squishing a
beast-man to jelly under one foot, and coolly Jimajin the Decisive and Unexcitable, his mind racing
at an incredible multiplicand of his usual
brainspeed, drew and loosed. Now the enormous
ursinoid wore both feathered shafts, one protrud-
ing from each ruined eye-socket.

Allayth laughed. No no, I am weeping. Nothing
is funny! This is all becoming irritating. So many
demands on me. Bear bare beer bore boor bear
begabee boogabee bugabear . . .

Though the blind beast roared and flailed and

stamped, the beast-man destroyed him and fell down shouting praise and thanks to Jimajin, calling him *tarf*: great chief. And he descended laughing to lead His People—his *almost*-people. Maybe he could help them evolve, using his chronograph and lots of psilocybin. First though he had to cut open the bear to see if it contained anything edible; locusts, for instance.

Somehow he stumbled and put his hand right into the dead beast's mouth and the dead teeth raked and hurt. Then all the beast-men were laughing and Jimajin the Brave no longer was, and he at last awoke from his mushroom-induced hallucination to find that he wore cuffs and chains and was ringed by loinclothed, spear-bearing men, men, not almost-men or beast-men. And standing over him laughing was their leader, and he was indeed a squat ugly hideous hairy beast-man.

Allayth had the fleeting thought that now things damned well were what they seemed, but he did not laugh.

12

Year 94: Even listening to my mother's diary
was illicit. Hearing these other tapes is Forbidden. I have become a thief; the thief of the
taped journals of others, our predecessors for
nearly a century. Ninety-four years! It is not
possible. Is it possible that I have the extraordinary promise they say I have? I do not
know; what is there for me to do, in this society? Far less possible is that which none dares
speak: al-Bah'ram's longevity. How old was
he when my grandfather left Earth, on this
very ship-become-"world"? No, he has
cheated and tricked. The man must have
cloned himself, and more than once! Or—
there is no al-Bah'ram. Only tapes . . .

—814 Sareed

The time of observation was clearly registered
in the scanner's memory. When he saw how long
it had been available, awaiting his attention, he
screamed his rage and self-accusation. All these
hours he had wasted, not even noticing the readout panel, much less thinking to glance at it.
Emissions! *Something, someone from space has
landed on my planet!*

From Earth? Surely. Where else? Well—many
other worlds must have been colonized by now.
Perhaps the limitations of distance and the barrier
of lightspeed had been circumvented over the
decades. (Centuries. Yes, centuries, he remembered and mentally corrected. Too many memories, crowding his head.) Nevertheless—surely
these visitors, the source of the emissions registered by his scanners and sensors, had come from
Earth. A message or messages had been sent back,
hadn't they?

Yes. He remembered. He had punished the sen-
der and sought to deflect the message, to bend the
message-carrying beam.

Hadn't it? They—he? He could not remember.
Could not be sure. How long ago had that been?
He was no longer certain. He remembered far too
much and never never enough. Had not some of
the crew dispatched message(s)?

*But why am I thinking about all this now, when
I must be about Allah's business—oh! Someone
has come.* From space, onto this planet. His
planet. A craft had come through space from Earth
after—how long? Was it a hundred years? No no,
more than that. Fifty years that is a million years?
He could not remember (too many memories). A
lot of years. Many many years, and his loyal ever-
alert Eyes had registered the emissions—nearly
fifty hours ago! Many hours! All these hours the
readout panel had been yellow, trying to attract
his attention, to tell him. Visitors or invaders had
come to the greatest project since Creation, the
largest observational laboratory in all the history
of humankind. *My Creation!* Arrival was nearly
fifty hours ago and he had not known, because he

had not happened to glance at his own accursed telltale.

I failed to notice. That is terrible, terrible. I must assign someone to improve the system. So many components are no longer functioning! What is wrong with these people? We must have everything inspected, tested. The Eyes, all scanners, the self-destruct implants, the Where are the technicians? I need an alarm bell or buzzer. I must have someone—oh. He remembered. *There is no one. There are only Allah and I and those animals; the mortals.*

But I must do something. Emissions! A visitor from Earth!

He frowned. *Suppose that in the intervening years centuries millenia they had lost—no no. That was not possible! The true faith must prevail on Earth as it did in Heaven. Too many memories!*

Help at last. Perhaps they have come to aid me, to relieve me in coping with all this terrible responsibility. Perhaps—

They might also have come to interfere! To tamper! Would they be able to grasp, with their small mortal minds, what he had done; the enormity of this accomplishment and the enormity of the task remaining? Would they in their mortal space-traveling techno-dependent simplicity be able to understand the utter necessity of his removal of all the others? All those deviants and questioners and malcontents who had crewed the ship-become-station; who had after all been mere subjects; tools?

Too many memories . . . Oh the responsibility!

The poor animalistic simplicity of the mortals and the necessity for his constant scrutiny and efforts to keep them unswervingly on the path to Allah; to keep them simple and yet aid them somewhat in surviving a planet stocked with DNA-adjusted, bioengineered creatures that re-created the conditions of time's dawn on Earth! The work, the labor, the enormous responsibility and too many too many memories . . .

What had brought on all this thinking, this—oh. The telltale. Emissions. A craft had come to his planet. From Earth, of course. To help? Perhaps—and yet possibly to interfere, interrupt and disrupt, deviating from his will and the will of Allah, which were the same.

Ah! He need not contact them yet, he remembered, not thinking that they too would have sensors and readouts, to report his emissions as his remaining equipment reported theirs. No need to contact . . . too many mem . . . He would observe them first! Of course. His greatest—or most useful, at any rate—creation would merely fly over them. Observe. Yes. He glanced down at himself to be sure. Yes. The exoskeletal control-feedback suit still encased him, glistening. He turned to the screen, the instrument-flanked screen, the chair with the helmet and so-sensitive waldo controls. He sat. He buttoned up his Eyes, slid his arms into the controls, set his hands into the controls. Every fingertip knew its place and was still capable of sensitive controlling of the Eyes. He made the screen come alive. He saw through its eyes, the eyes of the Eyes. Ah. Home again. A deep sigh of satisfaction escaped him as he soared.

King Dragon aroused, sprang off the cliff,

spread featherless wings stretching nine meters
from tip to tip. Despite his weight they rode the
air, caught him on a current of air, spread wide
and flapped, flapped. Up he rose and turned,
flapping and flapping. Other pterosaurs saw him,
and either fled because of his superior size or
followed because . . . because other pteranodons
frequently followed King Dragon. Because he was
King Dragon. The eyes and Eyes of Allah and
al-Bah'ram. *Malik-rukh*, they called him. Lord
roc: King Dragon! Ruler of the world. (No no no
. . . no ruler. Servant of Allah All-knowing.
Merely servant, Messenger and Eyes. Steward of
the world—a world. Yes. Allah's Own World. *Ajr:*
Heaven.)

King Dragon flew above the forests of the world,
and he flew with surprising speed on fingered,
clawed wings of leather.

He flapped and flew, soared and flapped. Below
great clarvids lofted up toward him, often draped
with the "dribblechin": vine/moss-imitating
lichen that appeared to be drooling down trees,
rather than growing up them. Dribble-lichen
then, the color of polished antimony. Below rose
and spread the umbrella-like tree called chittapel,
whose bark was astringent and of value.
Daruphytes clung to the trees, using them, growing from them in the eternal floral quest for the
sun. Here pillartrees grew and had gained control,
so that their height and shade created clearings in
which lurked twinerbitch. On flew King Dragon,
flapping and soaring. Now he passed over a great
sprawling twisty spidertree, little less handsome
than King Dragon. This one's endurance, and
patience, and re-rooting branches or aerial roots

had turned it into a whole thicket, all by itself. Bromeliads decorated vines and branches and the blooms of a snakerloo, each the color of fresh cinnamon, seemed to wave serpentinely at the source of the great shadow that flowed liquidly over it. Flapping, soaring.

He flapped and flew, soared and flapped. Reporting, seeing, reporting. Other pterodactyli, lesser pteranodons, avoided him or fled him while a few slavishly followed, flapping and soaring. For he was chief, king, Malik-rukh; *Pterodactylis Rex.* King Dragon, abroad on the business of God and Bah'ram.

He flew, in accord with the wishes and guidance of Allah and al-Bah'ram, to the designated area. A clearing surrounded by trees. Lesser ones were broken, and some branches as well. A stream nearby, He caught an updraft, settled onto it like a leaf on water, and soared over. His bright eyes darted, his implants sensed, recorded, reported to other eyes.

No emissions. No sign of life.

At the edge of the trees he lofted, almost forgetting—*so many memories, O Allah so many many memories Allah be merciful*—to lift above the trees. Only just clearing the ginkcoids lepidodendroids coniferales: clarvid chittapel pillartree daruphytes hangflowers strophanthic splicers. There was much of the planned on his planet, and must too that was purely stochastic. He lofted, flapped, soared briefly, banked in an ungainly aerial maneuver to swing and go sweeping back. Below was no movement. No emissions registered. No sign of life. Oh, several, but they were unimportant; lizards, serpents, a snuffling hyænodon.

Report visually, then. (Anger.)

The frightful shadow flowed liquidly over the clearing. A small spacecraft, designed to land vertically. It was dead. Overturned, bent and twisted. Trees broken. Spacecraft bent and broken. No emissions. Over that bright bauble flowed the dark ugly shadow, and beyond it. King Dragon banked, slipped and lost altitude and recovered in a ludicrously ungainly maneuver; lifted, turned, flapped. Returned. A monster aflight, aerodynamically unsound and biologically improbable; a zoological bastard. Swoop; glide; look, look, look. (Anger rising.) (Frustration: *Report!*)

Remains of a human organism. Gnawed and partially twined by twinerbitch. (A woman? Of course; see the pelvic girdle.) Off the bent and broken little spacecraft. Ruined. Dead. In advanced decay—a prodigiously swift process on God's Planet, Allah's world.

Spacecraft: fallen. Dead.

Former occupant: broken; dead.

King Dragon shuddered in air and dived, flapping hard, hissing. Almost, he crashed to the ground. Almost. Instead he snatched up a fat vomit-colored lizard and caught himself and, flapping wildly, rushed over the well decomposed and decomposing corpse of Cicada Lurie. Flapping, twisting, he rose above the stench, rose and rose. The lizard twisted in the clawed hands and listened to the screaming of King Dragon. Mind-red with rage.

Flapping, screaming its rage, it/he tore the lizard in half in . . . air and dropped the twitching pieces. He soared briefly, then flapped again, seeking action action in anger.

People—people, *real* people, not those skin-

clad animals that spawned such as mighty Raafar
and poor hideous Abdur—had come, in a shining
little spaceship from Earth—he was sure it was
from Earth, home, mother planet—and landed—
so the evidence indicated; not a crash landing but
disaster after—and stupidly been slain, slain, ship
crushed, felled, made useless, *killed*, by that eter-
nally accursed bear that should never have happened to begin with. (Tracks remained; scent remained or rather "scent", those traces which King
Dragon read, and registered, and reported) and
the ship was dead, the human (only a woman but
Allah moved in mysterious ways) was dead, dead,
and disappointment was rage was blind red rav-
ing ravening unreasoning reasonless raging ravening (Raven: deathbird, scavenger of battle-
fields) madness disappointment too many memories blind rage.

King Dragon flew, and flew, and another (much
smaller and pure zoological) pteranodon came
too close in its curiosity. It was raked, torn,
chomped, and sent flapping flopping crippled
wounded bleeding to the ground to become prey
for scavengers. And King Dragon flew on.

King Dragon flew over a village of those pitiful
mortal creatures Allah and Bah'ram deigned to
suffer to live (to no good reason) and shivered in
rage and desire to attack *suppressed suppressed*
winging on and saw a most handsome young
woman of that village. Sunning herself. Thinking
of nothing though spatterthinking of sexuality
and her arrogance in attractiveness. And yet that
was not what King Dragon saw for it/he was a
thing now ruled by rage rage unsuppressed al-
Bah'ramic rage and seeking a vent any vent for red

swirling tugging twisting unsuppressed rage.
King Dragon set wings, talons, arms, beak, and
dived and dived and turned that decorative adolescent of the community called Gizah into a
shrieking ruptured runneling red ruined jumble
of red ribbons and shrieking death death death

13

Year 94: 814 Sareed's journal, continued. I cannot curb this quest for knowledge, knowledge. It affects me as an "infection," that strange affliction of former times. It is a fever, a flame in my very blood. Do they not say what extraordinary promise I have? I can hardly live with myself for wanting to know more, more. Has *He* kept a log; journals?

—814 Sareed

Year 94: It has been five sleeps now since anyone has seen 814 Sareed. Poor Leilah is disconsolate. Queries filed to the Leader have not been answered. She says Sareed slipped out, during Exercise Period! He was driven by a terrible, evil thirst for knowledge, knowledge. Al-Bah'ram had clearly told us that there are things we are not to know; not meant to know. Why can some not accept this?

—809 Nural

They spoke Arabic. It was what Allayth thought of as "classical" or pure Arabic, which to him meant twenty-first century. He was able to handle it well enough to understand—mostly—and be

149

understood. Many pronunciations had changed.
He was unfamiliar with some words, and had to
back his way into their slang.

He did not know whether these people were
descended (indeed!—devolved!) from some who
had come down off the torus ship/station centuries ago, or had evolved from embryos *adjusted*
with recombinant DNA. They did not know either
and his questions made no sense to any of them.
He did anger them, and stopped asking questions
that indicated he was not one of them.

It was strange that they called the world Ajjer,
which he came to realize was a normal-enough
modification of *Ajr*: Heaven. They called this hellish planet Heaven!

It was strange too that the female captive's
name was Joharah, but only because to him that
meant the planet. "Jewel" was a normal enough
name for a woman, and was older than al-Islam.
Exit Jauhar then; enter Ajr—and Joharah. Except
that they usually pronounced it lazily, as just
Johara, without the final throaty-h sound.

They spoke of al-Bah'ram as if he were alive. As
if he were a god. Often the name/title replaced that
of *Allah*, God, in standard daily expression. "La
Illahilla Bah'ram" shocked him when one of his
captors avoided lizard bite and uttered the
thanksgiving formula: "There is no god but the
Bah'ram!" Had the long-dead expedition leader
become God, over the years?

They were surly and impatient with his queries.
He was slapped when he questioned "Bah'ramo
ah'alam": "The Bah'ram is all-knowing." It was
another ancient, standard Allah-formula. The

Bah'ram was all-knowing and was thanked when one avoided danger. What a hold that long-ago leader had over the ignorant, superstitious savages his people had become!

Allayth did not return the slap or even assume a truculent stance, although the other man was a youthful fellow captive, not one of the captors. He had slapped in religious shock-response.

("Slaves" and "slavers" were terms Allayth was not about to consider, despite indications.)

They spoke too of *Malik'rukh*/"maleek roc," the Messenger of Allah—or of the Bah'ram. Superstition, Allayth supposed. A particularly large pterodactyl, perhaps. Rhamphorhynchus was already of prodigiously overgrown size, here, with wings like sails. Whether translated as Lord Roc or King Dragon, the term obviously had no literal or even reality-based meaning.

He was a captive, not a slave. A captive.

But chained! Good lord, how primitive! He wore a length of chain taken from the back of the woman's collar. Collar!

On each wrist a heavy chafing cuff of hard leather. Boiled, he assumed. Each might as well have been iron or paracadmium. The cuffs were connected by that chain of clinking links. Bronze! About a meter long. It was bothersome, dangling, and when he sought to ease that by wrapping the nasty thing about his arm, he was railed at and cuffed and threatened with worse. When the captives slept, their feet were cuffed together. They were guarded. Five captives and nine captors, armed with spears and knives, almost swords. Those extra long knives did not seem too likely, but neither did a lot of other things. And a couple of them had bows and quivers of arrows. Those interested Jim Allayth. Those he could handle, crude and only of wood though they were.

Most of his companions wore what appeared to be leopard hides, paws, tails and all—except heads. They were soft, yellow-beige to white, and seemed well tanned.

He and his fellow captives were being taken to some place called Hajarazad. Savior's Rock? That was close. Freer/Savior Mountain, perhaps. It didn't matter. He had a hardly sane or likely vision of a city behind monolithic towers, guarded by draconic statuary. And spear-bearers, of course.

He particularly noticed the woman. She bore not a hint of a wrinkle, crinkle, or even nascent sag, although she hardly looked happy. (*So? Neither do I.*) He doubted she was as old as twenty. She was led by a chain attached to what appeared to be a bronze collar, and she moved with sinuous beauty. Her lithe body was more naked than not. Crucial areas were mostly covered most of the time. (Which was better than could be said for Allayth after two sleeps and just under three wake-periods; he was naked but for his boots. No one made fun, which made him proud. After a while. Circumcision was again out of vogue on Earth and surely part of their Islamic religion, here. But none seemed to notice that the oddest of their captives was even odder than that: he had no foreskin at all, and never had.)

She—Joharah/Johara—wore much jewelry and some of it was of good workmanship. He saw bronze, and shell, and non-gem stones the colors

of raspberry and claret and sky, and a few non-precious gemstones. She looked marvelous. She looked better by the hour, too. To all of them, he was sure, and was surprised that her captors laid no hands on her.

They ate well and he studied and mentally recorded which tubers and nut-fruit-things and fungi they ate, and which they avoided or seemed to. They ate meat and it was good. He was sick twice and had the runs for days—Terran days, that is; a full long day, on Ajjer. He attributed that to the planet and his constitution more than to the food. He walked and walked, with ice in his calves, and after a time that vanished. After that his calves developed and his buttocks tightened and the charley-horses in his thighs went away and stayed away. He contrived to exercise his arms, jingling and all. He let the others see him use only his right hand.

He lusted for her, of course. So did the others, captors and captives. So would any man, and a lot of women. She was the next thing to beautiful, was Johara of Kwait. True, she didn't show much in the way of personality or vivacity and he assumed an intelligence level lower than that of anyone he knew (—had known—) and a level of education below any he deemed sub-basic. None of that, though, had to do with lust. His fellow captives relieved themselves when they could, and Allayth assumed the others' thoughts were identical to his: Johara of Kwait.

He had been accustomed to eating three and a half times a day, at intervals not exceeding five hours, except for a daily six or seven hours' sleep, after which the eating cycle began again. These

people were not of Earth, and their planet's rotation bore no resemblance to Earth's. They seemed
to eat every six or seven hours and snack on this or
that now and again, if they passed something
nicely pluckable. Allayth felt sure they were
sleeping only every twenty or more hours during
daylight—and more, and longer, at night. His
head responded by aching and his system by
forming gas and ignoring anything approaching
regularity. He felt adjusted, but knew his system
wasn't. He awoke at the wrong times and was
sleepy at the wrong times. He wondered if it ever
would make the adjustment.

The chill of the nights bothered him a lot more
than it did these "native" Ajjeri, too. They had
made an accommodating adjustment to a planet
on which the temperature reached 38 or so every
day here in the temperate zone, and fell to ten or
fewer degrees during every one of the long, long
nights. Could it be their bodies that had accom-
modated? Could the adjustment to the planetary
constant now be genetic, racial? He did not know
if that was possible, and for days did not think
about its being a possible result of a genetically
engineered adjustment. During the nights he was
chilly when he kept moving and cold when he
was still, while they curled to sleep and seemed
not to suffer at all. At least the temperature never
came close to freezing. Down here under the
forest canopy, heat was partially stored. He felt
that in open country—if any existed on Ajjer!—
nighttime temp might well fall to freezing. Too,
the planet's axial tilt was minimal but definite.
That meant seasons. He wondered whether this
were summer or winter—make that "winter," on

Ajjer. Allayth was not about to ask that kind of question, not of this kind of companions!

Framing questions was hard. They seemed not to know anything about people with machinery or different clothing, tools, weaponry, transportation. On the other hand, Jim Allayth could not be sure that they understood what he was asking. He did learn to know direction—generally—by sun and moon; (the two outer ones were hardly a factor, especially down here in the trees), and was sure they were heading westward. Apparently though, Hajarazad was not the source of the emissions reported by *Cygnet* just before he and Cicada had stupidly set down so far away.

Besides, they did not like his questions. These primitives (?) obviously felt that everyone knew everything. Everyone probably did, he reflected, when there was so little to know. What had happened to knowledge? Had it been withheld? Were these the descendants of space travelers from Earth, or of adjusted fetuses?

Allayth had already asked enough to be considered stupid. No use making himself appear a halfwit, he decided, and stopped asking. He accepted, or tried to and pretended to, and observed.

On the second Ajjeran day—the seventh Terran day—they gave him clothing. He was grateful for the pouch and a bit of spotted, fulvous hide. He was not pleased to be forced to replace his boots with the local version. Without heeled footgear, he knew he would have to learn to walk differently. He began.

The squat, beastly leader took his boots and strutted in them. Allayth hoped those fine equhyde boots raised incredible bunions on the feet of the incredibly ugly creature. His name was Abdur and should have been Igor. He appeared to be the result of a bioengineering experiment gone wrong.

Maybe the whole bloody planet is.

They plodded through the rain forest. The captors were a long way from home. Allayth listened, and plodded, and thought and plotted. He heard the sounds of Ajjer and began to grow accustomed to them. He saw the pterodactyls—grossly overlarge—and the megatherium they slew for meat—and the diplodocus they tried to slay for that purpose. It departed wounded, angry, and yet fearful.

Allayth saw T. Rex, too. The sight was awesome, if not elevating or conducive to pleasant dreams. The monster they called Kingsaur was happy to accept the remains of their kill, the adolescent triceratops, while its mighty slayers ran like hell. Losing a man to the fifty-ton beast was ghastly, a horror. Yet . . . it was one of the captors, and Allayth was soon over personal feeling. *Eat 'em all*, he thought, *and we five will be free.*

And then what?

Though the tyrannosaur was a carnivore and the worst menace according to research sources, Allayth wondered nervously about the mother of that baby three-horn. That proved as needless as most worrying; they never saw her.

One captor walked out ahead, on point, and another to the side. Then paced Abdur, in his new boots. He led Johara by her neck-chain. The other captives followed, bunched, well watched. What they watched was Johara's backside. That was worse than unwise; it was torture. Better to look elsewhere. Not delivering oneself up to such torture, however, was at the edge of possibility's realm.

Allayth was asked few questions. He made no attempt to explain his origin. They probably wouldn't believe him, and that would bring more sneers and cuffs. If they did believe, the result might be worse. Who knew what superstitions these people had; what legends?

("What is your community?")

("Earth, by God!")

("Never heard of it and what has God to do with it? How far is it?")

("Farther than you can conceive of, you subliterate creep.")

(Slap. Kick.)

He took that, too. Allayth was learning. If they wanted to interpret his learning, his passivity as resignation and cowardice, fine. He wasn't resigned, and told himself he was not a coward. He did not know, of course. What opportunity had he ever had to discover whether he was brave?

That same subliterate creep slipped a funny mushroom into his dinner a few hours later. A jannfruit, they called it. The resident jinni promptly seized possession of Jim Allayth.

One of the hallucinations was just lovely. Somehow, the bearded Allayth knew that he was in Hajarazad. Swell place. Mighty walls surrounded him, the sort of walls that might ring an amphitheatre, an arena behind the mighty monolithic gates he had envisioned. From the walls jutted hideous statuary, so that saurian heads seemed to preside snarlingly over the arena.

Yes, arena. Thousands of subliterate creeps sat up there watching. Every one in a toga, snowy and flowing and smug. Romano-Ajjeri subliterates, betting, during a pleasant afternoon at the Games. It was all as likely as . . . as this planet!

In the arena: Jimajin Allayth. Heroically bearded, spear-armed. And Johara was there, lovely sweet so-desirable Johara of Kwait. Decor of dragon's teeth and pure gold flashed on her sinewy lithe psychotropic body, and she clutched a good-sized dagger. Hajarazad and psilocybin had contrived to "clothe" her so that both lovely breasts were nicely bared, and Jimajin was grateful.

Some sort of gigantic Thing menaced them. It was almost a triceratops but not quite, and he thought of it as a rhinosaurus, as if nomenclature mattered.

Lord Jimajin, superbly muscled and lithe as a cat with the confidence of a lion, stuck the thing five or seven times with his spear. Again and again he bravely intervened to save His Woman. Johara was worshipfully grateful.

Lithe as a . . . That reminded him, and he whistled up a bit of help.

The sabertooth tiger, long as two Allayths and sleek as . . . as Johara, tore hell out of the rhino-Thing and Lord Jimajin carved out its liver for the cat and he loved hell out of the incredibly grateful Johara and they lived happily ever after. The toga-clad creeps up in the stands turned thumbs up, too. Lord Jimajin simply attacked, woman by side, and sicced his loyal cat and incredibly grateful woman on them, and soon he was Emperor of Baghdad. That is, Hajarazad. Make it Rome.

Empress Johara fed him grapes. And pome-
granates. No mushrooms.

He returned to ugly reality shouting, caught,
hurting. They laughed while they cut him free of
the predatory vine's main portion. He was shaking all over and drenched with sweat. Hurting,
staring at the thing. At last he had made the ac-
quaintance of the twinerbitch.

"Wants a woman's touch," Abdur snarled, and
shoved Johara to her knees beside Allayth. When
Allayth started to move, he was booted back.
Double the insult; the boots were his own, or had
been.

"Be very still," she told him. "You know it will
hurt." Her voice was so soft it bordered on being
dull.

"It hurts already," he gasped. "What—what is
it? What happened?"

Huge eyes, deep and dark as wells looked into
at midnight and yet soft as puddles of melted
chocolate, stared into his. "You do not know?"

He shook his head. "It's a vine? Is it—is it *in*
me?"

"Hurry it up, there!"

Without glancing at the snarly captor, she returned to her work. While she freed him of nasty
little tendrils that really had pierced the skin on
his leg, she explained. He had to prompt her.
Johara could not believe that he had not experienced the twinerbitch, much less that he did not
even know of it. She also was not much of a talker.

The vine grew on the dark forest floor. The
shade and height of the pillartree, for instance,
created lovely beckoning clearings—but beware

the twinerbitch lurking at its base! It liked blood and was attracted by heat. Its capability was to send out shoots with impossible rapidity: tendrils that could grow as much as 35 centimeters in an hour, even less. Everyone knew it was dangerous to seek sleep within a meter of one. The little pink rhizoids went right into the skin, in the same way that some flora and such lichen as liverwort rooted themselves in the ground. It was necessary to cut the vine swiftly and cleanly, she explained, well away from the victim. Then each rhizoid ("tooth") had to be pulled out, straight out, with care. Else they broke off and infected. Yank them out while the parent vine still lived and they would "spit" toxin into the victim.

Wonderful. He wanted to remain with her and learn more from her—while looking at her, feeling her nearness—but that was not to be allowed. The leader of the captors led her personally, by her neck-chain. The others followed. Staring, naturally. It was torture, and the beastly ugly bastard in Allayth's boots very well knew it. Allayth hobbled now, his leg burning. So were his cheeks, for the others made it eminently clear that he was an idiot who knew less than a five-year-old child.

Eventually the burning sensation left his leg and he walked naturally while he took note of the Ajjeran forest around him. Anything to avoid looking at the womanly movements of Johara's semi-bare bottom or to engage in reality-testing. Just now an artful denial of fact was the best means of coping.

If a single hue or tint existed that was not represented in the algae and fungi of Ajjer, Allayth could not imagine what it might be. Here coiled

the purple-pink of clover and there the yellow of
aged gold edged with butter; here six hues of
azure and cerulean shading to cobalt beside turquoise and tourmaline; nestled against that chittapel was a lovely lacery of purest amethyst. Even
as he looked at it, his furry boot came down on
emerald and chrysoprase. Over there gastromyce-
tic puffballs hunched their shoulders, just under a
meter in diameter and the color of embarrassment. Trying to hide at the base of that hard-
wooded tree called clarvid were discomycetic
fungi in copper and plum and puce whose cups
were sufficient to accommodate his head and
more. Those ethereal almost-yellow lovelies,
dangling cheerily from the spidertree, were the
arboreal epiphytes called spirt. By now he knew
that during the long Ajjeran night, spirt emitted
an evanescent luminescence from its bulbs . . .
which also popped to gush a chlorous gas that
could knock out a human for an hour or more.
Long enough for a lurky twinerbitch to move in
for dinner.

Once the Hajar named Abdulassan stumbled
into a luridly crimson cup-fungus that discharged
its asci with a noise considerably louder than the
loudest fart Allayth had ever heard. Everyone
laughed at Abdulassan's jump and fortunately
did not notice Allayth's.

He learned about talsam. That big, bright-hued,
meaty fungus was so high in protein and so fleshy
that it was worth carrying—like a talisman,
talsam—for days. It was a fine refresher, which he
assumed must be loaded with the energizing vi-
tamin, B6.

So much fungi was more than important, he

knew, in reducing organic matter to simpler forms. The saprophytes worked thus on dead and decaying matter. Of that there was an abundance and more, beneath the sky-aspiring trees of Ajjer. By listening and observing he learned to identify two rhizomes whose bulbs were gloriously and nourishingly edible, and another with handsome potato-like bulbs that killed slowly and horribly.

Captive. Slave.

His disavowal of reality had aided him through the potentially devastating new fact of existence. Hours and sleeps later, surrounded by exotic beauty, he found the ability to swallow hard, face the word "slave," and begin to mobilize other coping efforts. Slave . . . Had Marco Polo been a captive, a slave? He couldn't remember. Did it matter?

As a slave, he did not have to worry or fight and decide in order to survive. As a slave he would be taken care of, and could observe and think and analyze. Did they have paper? Writing instruments? No matter; he could invent them for Ajjer. A slave who showed his . . . master . . . how to keep unforgettable records would be valuable indeed. Perhaps slavery was the perfect calling for a scholar. What a sociological observation he could make, while being housed, fed . . .

Perhaps inventing ink and writing would merit him a woman. He glanced at Johara's unconsciously busy backside. He swallowed and looked away. Not in embarrassment or anything approaching; he just could not stand the enticing sight.

They paused without making camp and despite his chains Musa swaggered up before Allayth.

Musa was young and nice looking, almost pretty. He was the one who watched Johara the most. Allayth, thinking, did not look up at his fellow slave.

"Such a clever slave," Musa said. "Pretend to know nothing of the twinerbitch so that *she* plucks them tenderly from your ugly leg."

"Umm," Allayth said. He was pondering this business about the Bah'ram, and had no time for Musa's machismatic posturing.

"You are a very clever fellow, aren't you— stupid child."

Allayth, seated, looked mildly up at the standing youth with his earring and his long-tailed breechclout. Musa's posture was pugnacious, challenging. He resembled a boy standing over a smaller boy he considered either smarter or luckier; his type knew little difference between the two, and disliked both. *Just chockfull of norepinephrine and begging to fight,* Allayth thought.

"Why challenge me, Musa? We are both captives." He lifted his hands with a succession of clinks. "Chained. We have no reason for trouble. They are the enemy. Neither of us gets Johara. They will."

"Do not speak her name, leather-chewer!"

Allayth shrugged. It was the old women who chewed leather to make it supple. Their captors were doing things about food. He had been insulted. The other captives were watching him and Musa.

"All right. I have no reason to quarrel with you, Musa. I'm busy thinking. Let me alone."

Musa sneered, naturally. "Thinking! Slaves do not think. We are slaves, leather-chewer."

"Do slavers prefer dangerous combative slaves or quiet ones who think?"

Those words brought laughter, from Hussayn and Abdulassan and Asghar and Johara. Musa rounded on her, naturally.

"You laugh at me, bare-titted whore of a slave who wags her tail for her captors?"

Allayth didn't think about it; if he had, he would never have risen and punched Musa. At that, he was calculating at some level; he feinted with his right and struck the younger man with his left, his better arm and fist. A nice solid punch to the jaw. Musa's teeth clacked and he fell down and Allayth emitted a yelp over his hurt hand and the jar to his shoulder and then the world went very silent. Many eyes stared at Jimajin Allayth. He was most aware of those of Johara and of Musa. The latter looked up at him from the ground.

14

Year 100! Today, our Bah'ram be He blessed addressed us all, every one, through every speaker in every compartment of every sector. I liked what he said, as everyone did. I was enthralled! The words of the Leader! Yet— something about his voice, his tones, made me nervous. Silly, silly. Who am I to judge God's spokesman; Creator of a Planet and Leader of us all? Merely 848 Jamsheed, longing to see what a planet is like. When will we be allowed to Go Down? There is *life* down there now, trees and microbes, and living things in the shallow seas. Life! Why not humanity? *He* says Jauhar is not ready for us and that we are not ready for Jauhar. It is true that some fear it, and do not want to leave this world. But this is not a *planet!*

—848 Jamsheed, Blue?

"He said mean things to me and you struck him."

"That's true."

"They hit you for it, and Abdur kicked you. You did nothing. And you had done nothing before, either. You were . . . meek. We thought you . . ." Johara did not finish.

"I know." He was quivering. Prickly and actually quivering! So great was his need with her standing over him, stooping. She had been about to say "We thought you were a coward," he was sure.

"You did nothing when Musa made an old woman of you."

The hyper-sexist term meant "insulted." Allayth nodded. "True, I did not. I was busy thinking. Musa's words didn't hurt me. I am bigger than his words."

She nodded slowly, absorbing that. "Thinking," she repeated. "Yet when he said mean things to me you struck him."

He said nothing, only looked at her. He did let her see a restrained smile. She continued silent, looking at him, and Allayth, being Allayth, had to fill the silence.

"Yes. That angered me. His calling me names, trying to pick a fight—that didn't disturb me because I didn't let it. *I* decided. You had no possibility even of deciding. You had to take what he said. That made me mad, so I punched the creep."

"You think . . . and decide when to be angry and when not to?"

In a way, he thought, *only in a way. I was chained and he looked strong, too.* But in the way of a man with a maid he said, "Yes."

"You fight for me. You would be my man?"

"Every man here would be your man, Joharah," he said, pronouncing her name the old way. "Or make you his woman, which is almost the same."

She looked around and her face took on an imperfect expression of hauteur. Mouth firmed, eyelids lowered halfway under slightly arched brows. The imperfection of the expression pleased him; it told him that Johara had not had much practice at looking snotty.

"Slaves," she said. "Hajar people-hunters, and slaves. Musa: a boy." And she looked at Allayth with an entirely different expression.

"All right. Yes, I would be your man, or have you be my woman. It isn't as if we can do anything about it, Johara. They have us. We are captives." He stabbed a finger at her without touching her, and accompanied the gesture with a sternly meaningful look. "Captives, Johara. Not slaves. Not—" He broke off. He would not add "Not yet."

The stone/bronze-age woman looked at him, thinking about that. At last she nodded. Glanced around. Met his eyes again. "I undertand. Yes. He who strikes Musa may next strike Abdur, and then the captive never becomes slave."

He managed not to groan. *She thinks I'm plotting a big attack.* Five prisoners in chains and eight captor-escorts, and he was going to jump Abdur! Not likely. "Uh . . . listen. Let me tell you about me, and thinking. One who strikes a fellow captive may be struck back by him, and will be punished by the Hajars. They, though, are armed. One who strikes a captor may be hurt, or worse. Don't get valor mixed up with heroics, Johara—or intelligence."

She thought of Raafar but she said, "I . . . do not understand."

"Yes you do. You just have trouble seeing the difference between bravery and heroics, and stupidity. Between cowardice and thoughtful behavior."

"Thoughtful . . . behavior."

"Yes." It occurred to him that she might well be about to break the lovely spell, this unexpected conversation, by saying something truly ignorant. He did not want that to happen. (Terran) days and days had passed. Pure biological need was on him, the need called rut, and Johara was more than attractive. He wanted her. He did not care to learn that she was a dolt. So he said more, before she could.

"Johara. Abdur is looking this way and we're about to be interrupted. Listen. If anything . . . unusual happens, anything, you have a good chance of getting away. Just grab the chain to your neck, yank it, and run. See, if anything happens, the unexpected, Abdur won't be alert to trying to keep a tight grip on your chain." He had nearly said "leash."

She shrugged, which made him squeeze his eyes shut. *Allahuma!*

"This I have thought of, but I already know that for me to run into the woods alone will not save me. You will make this 'something happen,' and you will be my man? What is your name?"

"Jim."

"Stop that talking! Get away from him!"

"Zheem?"

"Yes. Jim Allayth."

She smiled. "Of course! Jim the Lion! You will make something happen, Jim al-Layth, *nuzhat al-fuad.*" She straightened. Abdur, who had started forward behind her after his shouts, paused. He watched, though, to be sure she would obey.

Allayth squeezed his eyes shut. She still thought he was going to do a big number on Abdur and the two of them would run into the forest and live happily every after. "Get away from me, kurrat al-ayn," the mighty lion said, into her Oz-like fantasy.

She had broken his name into its components. He had not thought of its meaning that way for a long, long time. His old friend Ahmed Allomda had not been a village headman, omda; Allayth's name came from al-Layth, the Lion, or Lyon. He had nearly forgotten. It meant nothing, it was just his name. Naturally it meant a lot to primit—to these people. And she had called him darling— "delight of my vitals," in old Arabic—and he had called her the same: "coolth of eye," which also translated more easily as darling.

I have fought for her, he mused while Johara departed. *O Allah, O my God! What a fine primitive man I am! What chivalry! A maiden insulted, and so I fought. (Fought? I punched the bastard; a damned good punch. He took it, too. No shit or sass from him, since, with that bruise on his pretty jaw!) And she is a primitive woman. I fought for her, defended her even though it was against words only, therefore I am her man. Nuzhat al-fuad and kurrat al-ayn! Jim the Lion! O my God. Yes, your servant Jimajin remembers the meaning of the old word* macho, *in whatever language it was—Italiyis? Espanish?*

The ridiculous—or horrible, or ugly, or marvelous—part of it was that he knew he would do it again. He would indeed fight for her.

Even so, he sneered at himself for that—and wondered if he would be so motivated if he weren't so damned horny.

That afternoon poor Musa lost his head and made a direct grabbing attack on Johara, practically slavering, and Abdur beat the snot out of him. Allayth sympathized with poor Musa—and enjoyed the scene.

The swampy lake did not stink, exactly. It did exude an odor, and the odor was not the most pleasant. It was a combination of stale and long-standing water, and rot, and humidity. The lake lay not placid, but dead as an enormous puddled streak of cold molasses. It was far from that viscid, of course; it did look so. This standing body of stagnant water within the Ajjeran forest did not merit any of the lovely old words used to describe water; it was not azure, or pellucid, or cerulean or even emerald. It was murky and mucky, beginning as swamp and running out and out until it was too deep for the trees to continue to grow in it. Mucky, soupy, thick-looking. Here and there it erupted a twisty tree or water-dwelling plant or "plant." Allayth saw a water snake, a normal-sized ugly rearing its baby's fist of a head above the water and leaving a ripply wake as it zoomed away from the noisy two-legged invaders of its shore line territory.

Here and there the broad but forest-bound lake was blinding glass, where sunlight sneaked around or between trees to strike it directly. Things like cat-tails wriggled up around its perimeter and yet they were unlike cat-tails. Pre-reeds, of the simplest form. There were too the ubiquitous ferns, and tilted, arthritic trees. They hung over that dark and gravid water not like sentinels but like cripples come down to the water's edge in quest of miraculous cure.

Lake Lourdes, Allayth thought, staring side-

wise as they were forced along the shore. Their
captors were looking for something, along this
marshy edge of forest-surrounded lake that covered hectares; square kilometers and square kilometers. Beyond the far shore reared mist-
shrouded trees like buttes and towers.

They found what they sought: boats. Two,
which they had left here when they came ranging
from Hajarazad. Allayth swallowed. Somehow
crossing that lake was a most unpleasant pros-
pect; not just a step closer to real slavery, but the
crossing of a mighty big moat.

With only a little chatter, Abdur decided to
send over one boat containing two men. One captive, and one captor: Hussayn and Mabahr. The
others, four prisoners in chains and seven
human-hunters under arms, waited in boredon.
Watching two men row across a broad lake. Wait-

ing. For what?—for that damned little boat to reach the far side. Judging from the apparent size of the trees, that was over a kilometer away. At least the lake wasn't nearly as broad as it was long.

The boat covered the distance. The two ascended the bank, and the Hajar turned to wave his long almost-sword knife.

With a grunt, Abdur turned to look at his little company. His finger stabbed, then again, again. Abdulassan and Allayth and Saryd and Johara. The two Hajars he had selected prodded the two chosen prisoners into the second boat. Warped wood, and lianas, gnd bark and . . . sap, or some gelatinous stuff. Allayth and one Hajar were expected to row. The other sat astern and looked vigilant. Johara, up forward, just sat.

Chains clinking, Allayth rowed and was cursed when he bumbled out of rhythm with Abdulassan. Johara had worn a fearful look and he was glad his back was to her. He didn't look at anything. He just rowed. It grew old very quickly. His back and arms began complaining and then his hands, which had never done much to toughen their palms. After awhile his back began to flame. Humidity hugged them in a soggy bail sweat. After another while his back's hurting dulled into an ache he could control, in a way. He kept it steady, bent. That was better than intermittent relief followed by fresh stabs or flameups of pain.

On and on it went, and now it was not just that he wasn't looking at anything; he saw nothing. Dull-eyed, bent, he rowed and tried not to think about galley slaves.

A week or ten later they reached the other side and Jim Allayth groaned when he boated his oar and straightened. Now that hurt! Saryd, looking very happy, watched Abdulassan go ashore. He ordered Johara out. The other Hajar stood on marshy land, ready. The boat rocked slurpily as she left it. Allayth did not turn to look. He could imagine the marvelous sight of her debarking, and that was bad enough. Then the boat was still, and Saryd gestured. Allayth, with exaggerated care fueled by nervousness, rose half-crouching. He turned with slow and deliberate movements.

Ashore, well back from the water's edge, Mabahr stood with ready spear. Abdulassan, closer, sort of leaned on his bow while he watched Allayth. Allayth went ashore without falling. He had never so much as seen a boat before.

"*Mabahrr!*" Abdur bellowed, and Allayth was sure he saw the ugly Hajar leader's mouth move just before he heard the words. "*Return with the boat! Abdulassan: back well away from them and keep your bow ready. Keep them together. Saryd: return with the other boat!*"

"Dung," Mabahr snarled, and came down to the water's edge. A water snake plopped and streaked away. The man paid little attention.

We all could have crossed at once, dummy, Allayth mused. *Why all this ritual? What was wrong with these dummies? Were we decoys for something? Bait?*

Abdulassan had Hussayn and Johara join Allayth near the waterline, where they had less chance of plunging into trees and junk-shrubs and getting away into the forest. Allayth watched the retreating boats, not Abdulassan. His peripheral vision, though, apprised him of the man's stepping several paces away, inland. His

bow was strung an an arrow lay in place, though
loosely held. They watched the two boats go back,
well separated. It took a long time.

Objectively, forty minutes or so, Allayth
thought. *Subjectively to those poor bastards rowing: a week or ten!* Sweat still ran down his body.

*Whatever his reason for all this back-and-
forthing delay,* Allayth reflected, *ole Abdur
hasn't been intelligent about it. Over there: two
prisoners and seven captors. Over here, one
watches three. If we had any gumption we'd scat-
ter slowly, and try jumping Abdulassan.*

His heartbeat eased into a lower gear and began
to thump. His brain was working just as hard. It
became a sort of underlying drumbeat to the
cacophonous thoughts: *Try it, try it.*

On the far shore, the nine men disposed themselves in the two boats. They commenced rowing.
Try it, try it, try it. Allayth saw that the tired Saryd
and Mabahr were shirking, coasting on the efforts
of the others. Good!

"Hussayn," he said very quietly, staring at the
far boats. "Wait a while after I stop talking. Then
move a pace away and back. Slowly. Wait awhile,
then ease another pace. Not toward Abdulassan,
and don't look at him. Johara: notice something
you want to pick up, a long pace from me,
downshore."

His heartbeat was thunder and his armpits
prickled. Sweat broke out on him anew, a new
kind of sweat.

The boats moved while the four stared. Thump
. . . thump . . . the oars said, and thumpathump-
athumpa, Allayth's heart raced. Johara moved
away from him to squat and take up a pebble that

she seemed to find enthralling. A slight sound behind him and on his other side told the Earthman that Hussayn had moved his pace away. *Stare at the boats, Abdulassan. The boats, the boats* . . .

Abdulassan said nothing. They stood staring dully at dullness. A placid boat on a placid lake.

Painted ship on a painted sea, Allayth thought, watching the approach of the boats, and was unable to remember where the line came from. The craft were well separated. By now so were he and Johara and Hussayn.

All in an instant, pandemonic disaster showed why Abdur had taken such time-consuming precautions, and that they had been for naught, and that the boats were not sufficiently well separated at that. The lake serpent erupted without any sort of warning. It came up like an explosion from the depths of the water, and its size was prodigious. Water flew high and far amid incredible sound as the whipping cable of a tan-and-brown-scaled, obscenely yellow-bellied body appeared. Thicker than a very fat man, long as an Ajjeran tree. A loop arose far and another came up directly under Abdur's boat, which was hoisted nearly a meter above the lake before it slipped sidewise. Abdur and the other occupants managed a few yells and shrieks and even a wild spear-slash before they were gone. So much for his having used others as bait.

The creature's head appeared simultaneously, seven or eight meters away. It bore down on the other boat, which it must have seen or sensed from below. Allayth saw ridiculously small flippers and a row of flexible dorsal fins and a slim,

ugly snout-horn or sensor, and great luminous
eyes of gold barred with black. And rows and
rows of teeth long as fingers and sharp as daggers.

Men began yelling, and only later did Allayth
realize that one of them was he.

The grossly overgrown serpent moved through
the water faster than men could row or use their
bows. Behind that rushing head dark water
streamed in undulant varicolored lines. Somehow those in the second boat contrived to escape
that first charge, slamming spears and oars into
the beast so that it swerved, seeming to roll in an
impossibly long barrel. Water boiled and
splashed white and scales flashed refulgently in
horrid beauty. A great undulant mass of body
came up and snapped at the boat's side. An oar
broke and the craft lurched under an impact Allayth heard aloud. Cleverly chained together,
both captives went over the low boat's side and
vanished.

One Hajar was caught in a twisting roll of serpentine body. Even as he was squeezed and then
dashed below the surface, he was driving and
pounding his broken oar into the creature's side,
piercing that mass of destruction. The fourth man,
alone in the little boat, used his spear as a lance
and tried to stave off the monster. Water splashed
high and white while scales on that twisting body
scintillated like mail. The beast itself made no
sound, though the noise of churning water was
horrific. About to die and knowing it, desperate,
the last of the nine men thrust his long knife
directly into the reptile's cavernous mouth.

It kept coming, so that the knife and arm went in
and in, and then head.

That swiftly the ghastly massacre on the lake was over. Only then did Allayth consider himself and realize that the monster might swerve and come for him and his companions ashore. Evan as he began turning toward Abdulassan, that thought was superseded: *Abdulassan can't hold us. He'll listen to reason . . .*

That thought was superseded, too. The stricken Abdulassan was staring out on the lake. His bow was forgotten, arrow still nocked; forgotten too were the three captives. The Hajar was frozen, staring, and for the moment, mindless. He stood several paces up the shore, nearer the trees. To Allayth's right as he turned was Johara, a step closer to the water than he, and three paces from him. A couple of meters leftward and behind him, nearer Abdulassan, stood Hussayn. He had watched as the others had done, soundless, fixedly glaring in horror. Allayth's first movement drew his gaze, and freed his brain.

The moment Allayth started to turn, Hussayn ceased looking at him. He wheeled and wasted time snatching up a whitened chunk of driftwood to use as a club. Then he drove at Abdulassan—whose peripheral vision had caught the movements. Johara, too, spun and started inshore, toward the man three meters away.

Allayth had to forget all thoughts of trying to reason with the Hajar. They had understood his instructions, and assumed he meant to attack Abdullassan. Obviously the time was right now, and they were charging. He must.

Hussayn, with a meter of chain, dangling between his wrists to serve as a weapon, should not have taken time to pick up a club. Abdulassan had to turn only a few centimeters to his right, lifting his bow, and whip the other hand to the string. Impending attack enabled him to move faster than any man should have been able. He snapped an arrow into the rushing man at a distance of less than two meters.

Hussayn's momentum drove him on. In his falling, his chains clanked into Abdulassan's shins; the driftwood club accomplished nothing.

The Hajar staggered, saw now the charging Allayth, and snatched forth another arrow rather than his long-knife. Allayth was already swinging back both arms over his right shoulder. He reversed direction of that swing while Abdulassan laid arrow to bow-hand and then to string. As he pulled, Allayth's joined hands were rushing around and forward, trailing a doubled length of chain. It flashed, sweeping at the Hajar's face. In the act of loosing an arrow, he tried to duck. Allayth, the wildness of his movements and the chain's tug upsetting his equilibrium, began falling. The bowstring twanged, weakly. The chain connected with a clinking thump not as loud as Abdulassan's scream, and Allayth fell.

He wallowed, scrambling, half-crawling, cursing.

Because he had to get up, he got up, onto his knees, but his chain was caught and pulled him off-balance. He fell cursing and scrambled, half-crawling, his heart working at pounding out a hole in his chest. He expected the shock of a sword-cut or an arrow impact at any instant. With all his grounded strength he hurled himself sidewise and away from Abdulassan, meanwhile yanking at the chain with both hands. It came free and banged his leg. That not only hurt, it smeared and spattered his leg with blood that was not his.

Rolling over again, wincing at the new chain bites at his calf, Allayth saw about getting himself vertical. He did. And stared, shocked.

Abdulassan was a mess. The chain had ruined his mouth and his nose and the knife Johara was sticking into him—his own—was ruining his guts. There was lots of blood, bright and shining wetly. Her mass of rather stringy, trying-to-curl black hair all over her face and shoulders and one side of her chest, she looked up at Allayth. She was panting and blood was splashed up her right arm to the elbow.

"That's . . . probably enough," he said, while his knees kept trying to convince him that they wanted to bend at least 45 degrees.

She stared blankly at him. "He was moving. I thought he would kill you while you were down—"

She looked down at what she had been doing. At Abdulassan. At her forearm. She croaked an ugly little throaty noise and a great seismic shudder ran all over her and then she vomited all over the mess she and Allayth had made of their former captor.

Allayth was glad, even while his stomach lurched. At least her reaction told him that her repeated stabbing of the Hajar had been a blind response to adrenaline and fear and hysteria and her captivity and—fear for him? Then he remembered something else, and whirled to look out on the lake.

A boat floated, and some pieces of wood, and part of a man. Only part. Lake Lourdes again; Lake

Placid again. The water-monster had defended its territory and lunched or dined as well, and had submerged for a nice siesta. So much for seven slavers and three innocents. Well, maybe his fellow captives hadn't been so innocent, Jimajin Allayth thought, hopefully.

The next memory came, and he turned to go to poor old Hussayn. He lay on his side, partly curled, with both hands on the shaft of the arrow in his neck. The hands were locked, and Hussayn's eyes were wide and staring. His chest wasn't moving.

Allayth sighed. "Nice shot, Abdulassan, dammit."

He knew that had he moved faster, really been the macho hero and charged, he would have taken that arrow and maybe it would be Hussayn who was standing here—free! *We're free! I'm free, and I even got the girl. I must have done—we're the only ones left alive!*

Just then Johara screamed.

He had the sinking stomach sensation when he saw that she was looking past him, at the lake. He looked that way. The water had gone all murky again. It remained placid. No, she had screamed at what she saw on the far shore.

At this distance Allayth could see magnificence. Stone-age, barbaric magnificence of physical construction. And threat. And even as far away as the man was, Allayth could see that there was something wrong. His head was wrong.

The man was tall and just superlatively built. The usual skins covered his feet, lower legs and loins, with the tail dangling behind. Another hide was slung behind him, too, from his shoulders, so

that it framed that beautifully muscled body. A cloak formed of the hide of a truly huge spotted animal. Was that the beast's head on his hip, feline? Allayth thought so. And that ax! The man across the lake held it aloft, brandished and waving—a bludgeon of knotty, twisty mica-flashing stone far too big for one-handed wielding. Yet its haft was short; it was not a two-handed weapon. In his other fist the big man brandished both a thick spear as tall as he *and* a big, only slightly convex shield.

"JOHARAAAHH!" he bawled, and the voice was throaty and awful and Allayth could see that it issued from a mouth that was *wrong*.

The man had something badly wrong with the whole side of his face. It began with his scalp, for he wore his jet hair long while on that side Allayth could see the gleam of hairless scalp.

Behind him, Johara was babbling and whimpering. He backed to her. Even across a lake a kilometer and more wide, Allayth was unable to turn from the big, big man with the big, big weapons. Beside the trembling woman, he asked the identity of the other man. Twice he asked her, and then clamped her arm and twitched it to break her spell of hysteria.

"Johara! Who is that? Why—"

"Raafar," she said stuttering, and her voice broke. "Raafar Saurslayer of my people, of Kwait. He is hideous!"

"I can barely see—"

"He is! He is! He *is!*"

"JO-OHAAARAAAHH!" Raafar was a horror-voice with a built-in microphone.

"What . . . does he want?"

"Me!"

Allayth nodded. So he had assumed. He had just needed to hear it, want to or not. Thank God for the lake! Here he stood with someone else's woman—and that someone else looked like a product of Viktor Frankenstein's laboratory. Huge. Mighty. Hideous. Raafar looked man enough and mean enough to have waded into that bear and had him for dinner, in bite-sized bits.

"J . . . ohara? Is he . . . your husband? Your father?"

"No! Oh we have got to RUN!"

"Your . . . brother?"

"No! No!"

"Jo-ohaaaraaahhh . . ."

"You don't want to go back to Kwait?"

"No! No!"

"Get yourself together. He isn't coming across that lake."

"He will! He will! I know he will. He is Raafar. Any other man with half his head torn off would have been happy to die!"

"Umm. Agreed. He is not coming right away, though. Think! He has the choice of building a boat or raft or taking a long, long walk." *Or stirring up the water to try to coax that overturned boat in to him,* Allayth reflected. *Or . . . swimming out to it. He'd have to leave the ax . . . So what? He still looks big enough to handle us and six others.*

Raafar could be as close as . . . less than two hours.

"All right, we'll put him out of sight, at least. Listen! Gather up your chain. Hold it to you in one arm. Keep the dagger—wipe it, oh please wipe it!"

Overcoming the distasteful operation amid so much blood, he stripped off the Hajar's long knife-almost-sword, and then his quiver. He had to pry the bow out of the dead hand. Raafar called again. At least he was not yet taking any sort of action. Allayth glanced at him, then upward. He thought west was to the right.

He did something awful. He went to Hussayn and, with some difficulty, retrieved the arrow that had killed the man. Allayth thought he could use the bow, but he certainly knew nothing of choosing wood and making arrows and fleching then, and he wasn't all that long on patience either. Hurrying down to the very edge of the water, he plucked from the reeds there the arrow Abdulassan had tried to put into him.

"All right, let's go. Into the forest. Stay close. Once we are well out of his sight, we'll get rid of the chains. Is west to the right?"

She hefted a hand as if to make sure of right. "Yes." She still trembled.

"Good. Let him see us seeming to cut left, toward the long end of the lake."

"Cut?"

"Come on!"

15

Year 100: I am tired of this! I have petitioned
him again and again, and this time my wording was strong, and I sent it *around* the Captain, His damned appointed warden, rather
than Through Proper Channels!
                              —848 Jamsheed, BLUE!

Year 100: Everyone is wondering what has
become of Jamsheed. No one had seen him for
days. The Captain says that he knows nothing, and the Leader says nothing. Some of
us are beginning to wonder, and talk. Yet we
must do so in secret. What sort of society have
we built here, anyhow?
                              —1013Abdul, BLUE!

After several minutes of making their way
through the deep-shadowed haven of the forest,
Allayth looked back. He could see only forest. Not
trees; forest. An amalgam of trees and shrubs and
lichen and fungi, all as if bound together by vines.
He brought Johara to a stop. She was more than
reluctant.
"Turn westward."
She looked at him. Started to speak. Bit her lip.

Nodded, turned, and pointed. He had not seen her glance up, but they went that way, around a tree big enough to serve as *Cygnet's* mausoleum, trailing vines that had bloated to the thickness of Allayth's wrist. The chains were a liability and their jingle was twice as bothersome, now that they were no longer captives. He endured it for an hour or so anyhow, knowing that she was in genuine fear. They came to one of those lovely inexplicable clearings that just seemed to occur, and started out into the tall grass of a broad veldt.

That was when they heard the shrieking roar. They stopped, and saw the grazing triceratpops only because it jerked up its ugly head.

"Bumblecow." She caught at his hand and he took hers willingly. "Did bumblecow make that sound?"

"No. See!"

He saw. He and Johara did not stay to see more: the encounter between old three-horn the well-armed and- armored herbivore and its attacker— a genuine beautifully sinuous hideously formidable gold-plated card-carrying satertooth tiger.

It isn't real, Jim Allayth thought, proceeding elsewhere at speed. *I didn't see that. It isn't possible.*

Then: *What a twisted sadistic idiot it took to create this world—deliberately! Thank God it's so sparsely populated with these nightmare things. During this period on Earth, they must have been practically falling over each other!*

And a few dekameters later: *But never before a planet called Heaven was there a battle between a triceratops of the Cretaceous and a sabertooth of the . . . whenever it was; a lot later. —And while humans watched, yet!*

After another kilometer of increasingly breath-less broken-field rushing, bearing weapons and wearing chains, they came to a stream. This was a gentle brook: a lazy shallow stream. Clear water played giggling over stones ranging from pebbles to really big chunks of granite that reared up dry and usually white as old bone. He caught her hand again.

"Johara. We stop here."

She whirled on him with a face gone all full of fear again. "Raafar—"

"Listen. He may follow and he may not. If he does, however he handles that lake it will take him a long time. We will make better time without these chains. Too, we'll be a lot safer, free of them. Better able to defend ourselves. We need to—"

"Only a little way farther. I fear him. I fled him, alone."

He nodded, studying her face. "You hate him that much."

"No!" She shook her head and hair flew—and her chain clinked. "I *fear* him." She tugged at his hand. "The chains will not take long. But it will not take long to go farther, either."

"Well—"

"We could cross the stream," she said excitedly. She glanced that way. "If we could get into the water without leaving tracks at the water's edge, and then across . . ."

"Yes. Good—very good! All right, we'll do that first—look! See that rocky shelf that juts out over the stream. It isn't too high . . . we go out on it, carefully, and drop onto that big white stone in the water. The smooth boulder, see? All right. Then we cross over to the other bank. And get these chains off."

She agreed, and they did that, with care and nervousness and such consummate ease that the whole crossing was commonplace, despite their chains and his unaccustomed burdens: sheathed long-knife, quiver, bow. An excrescence of stone hurt his heel, too, through the uniformly-soled hide boot he wore. At least the boot wasn't pierced. A long long vine dangled over the water, as if seeking a drink.

"Wait," he said, catching her elbow. "Take hold of the vine as high as you can reach, and hang on. I'll push you hard, and you let go only when you're well up the bank. That way we leave no tracks at water's edge."

"Oh! Yes!"

They did that. He enjoyed pushing her. She dropped lightly on the bank, and the vine took its time coming back. It hung only a little lower, now. Allayth tossed his bow over to her, and did his best to get up enough swing to join her. He swung short, and let the vine return him to the big stone.

"Again," she said. "Swing up your feet and I will catch you."

Doing that got him a rope burn on the thigh and a mild one in the palm. But they had crossed the stream without leaving tracks in the soft soil at water's edge on either side, and that made her happy. He still could not believe that Raafar would follow. *All* they had to do, Allayth assumed, was make their way ever westward and eventually they would find some sign of the source of the emissions Cygnet had reported—or be found by those people.

That was all.

Now Johara wanted to move out of sight of the bank they had quit, although she knew full well that if Raafar did come he had to be two hours behind, at least, and more likely farther back than that. Allayth went along. Then she wanted to go farther, just a little farther, in among those somber shadows and calm giants of the Ajjeran rain forest.

"No."

She gazed at him with large dark eyes.

"No, Johara. Now we take off the chains."

She looked at him, a lovely coppery primitive of twenty or so, lean of face and slim of figure, rather broad of shoulder and covered with what appeared to be a half-kilo of jewelry. Big, almost-black eyes gazed into his, and he felt himself ready to topple into those moonless wells. She nodded.

"Yes, al-Layth. All right. This collar will not be difficult for you—it is just impossible for me. See."

She turned her back and one hand swept her mass of hair up and aside. He gazed on lovely bare back, a lighter shade than the rest of her, and on that most vulnerable and ever erotic feminine area, her nape. It was not really marred by the bronze collar. He swallowed and discovered that his hands had gone trembly.

The collar curled into a closed loop at either end. These, molded to twist easily over each other, formed a cylinder about three centimeters long. Into it had been thrust a much smaller version of the same ring-ended loop. Through those rings in turn a chink-pin had been fitted, tightly. It curved into a hook at its bottom. A form-fit, bent screw. Unthreaded, he discovered, as he worked it up and out. While it was easy for him, it would have been impossible for her, or nearly. She'd have needed privacy and lots of time and patience—and an ability to withstand the strain to her arms. Unless she had simply turned the collar around. Maybe she hadn't thought of that.

He got it off, and discovered the lumps inside the collar. No. One would try to turn it but once!

Johara was uncollared. She turned, with a sigh, to face him. She rubbed her neck with both hands. It was marked.

"We could have done this a long time ago," he said. "It only took a minute."

She looked down girlishly. "I know. I was afraid. I still am. He followed so far! You see what a tracker he is. No one is better at tracking than Raafar—and he has the patience of a constrictor."

He thought of that poor creature with the spectacularly beautiful body and spectacularly ruined face, and the voice that had bellowed her name again and again, and Allayth's back crawled. Yuh, Such a man had patience, all right.

"Yes." He held up his wrists with a clink of chain. "All I have needed is a good sharp blade, of course. The cuffs are leather, and a metal plate is sewn in to hold the ring of the chain. Hmmmm . . . I'll bet I can cut out the chain, and keep the cuffs as bracers."

"Oh yes. You should have bronze, though, at the very least. You will wear gold, al-Layth. You will see."

With her help, he removed the chains and kept the bands of leather. She was close and her odor was not unpleasant. Neither was her touch and her hair wanted hands in it. He felt the tremors in his belly; she saw those of his hands. She looked up and their gazes met. The chains dropped. A few links hit his soft-booted foot. It hurt. He showed nothing, and did not move. She was about ten centimeters away.

"We are free," she murmured, "Jim the Lion."

"We've always been free. But now we aren't chained any more."

She blinked, and the edges of her mouth tilted up just a little. "You are like Sai," she murmured, and then her face clouded. "We are not free of Raafar."

He did not give a damn about that, not right now. His hands slid onto her hips, exerted a little pressure, and she came against him. He did not have to show her how to kiss.

The kiss was interrupted by the sound of the

flapping of huge leathery wings. Hanging onto Johara, Allayth looked up to see no less than a dragon; what had to be the grandfather of all pterodactyls. The hideous creature seemed uninterested in them, though, and flapped and soared on eastward. It vanished quickly behind a horizon of treetops.

He decided not to pursue his and Johara's obvious arousal. He had waited; he could continue to wait. Acceding to pure sensation could be most dangerous indeed, on Ajjer. That he had already learned. He kissed her forehead and eased away from the breast that seemed trying to burn a hole in his bare chest.

"Are those good to eat?"

"Of course," she said, looking at the yellow-and-beige mushrooms he indicated, five of them, about fist-size. They were trying to hide beneath an intricately twisted spidertree, one of those nightmare things from a forest of Oz.

"Let's have one," he said. And while they did: "Why does he follow you?"

She looked away, chewing. "If I tell you all of it, my lion may think less of me."

Not for awhile, he thought, but he considered. "Then we will walk some more, my lioness."

She looked suddenly troubled. "We will not leave the chains here to be found!"

He grinned and shook his head over that, but he understood. Staying very close to each other now, carrying the chains that seemed less heavy without the psychological weight of bondage, they fared on through the rain forest of Ajjer. Westward. She pointed up to a diaphanously blue aerophyte, and told him that the floating plant glowed at night. Love's Brand, they called it. The chirophytes with the x-shaped white blossoms, so delicate and pretty, were well equipped with clawlike roots to dig into the soil—or skin, she pointed out, accepting that he knew little. Some such "handplants" actually pierced trees, and became hosts for hangflowers. She showed him one of those handsome yellow bromeliads, sunnily blooming well above head height. He plucked it for her hair and received a look to jelly knees.

That sprawling thicket was a single spidertree, its aerial roots having spread and then re-spread its perimeter until it could have contained a fair-sized house.

They moved westward and he did not ask her about Raafar. He did ask question after question. She replied willingly. Her answers increased both his knowledge and his confusion.

Ahead of them, behind them, all about them sprawled herbiage in three dozen shades of green and a score of other hues. More than a score. That many-eye alone contained two shades of green, one *weird*, as well as red, blue, and white. Humus thrust up its fragile fungi, obviously modified to provide much food on this planet: fungiforms preferred the dark here, but did not demand coolth as they did normally—that is, on Earth. The towering over all of the trees was a constant, like the clear azure and opalescent sky they nearly blotted from sight. Lichen darkened them, dangled from them, bulged or seemed to bubble on their boles. Deep, deep was the shade in indigo and charcoal and black, and there were the mushrooms and blossoms most pallid and yet delicately lovely. Serpentine vines crossed and crisscrossed, twined and intertwined, braided and looped and wound, writhed and looped over the ground and up trees in quest of the sun. Here and there a stout tree's sturdy-looking branch dangled, held aloft only by the vines that had murdered it. Now and again a tree stood dead and growing pale, or had tried to fall only to be propped by sturdy neighbors, or lay dead and whitening even while feeing other life in a dozen visible forms. And Allayth gained in knowledge and in confusion, if that could be called gain.

What she knew was wonderful, and there were explanations. What she did not know was maddening. Knowledge and delight flamed in him even while frustration gnawed.

She knew nothing of other worlds and had no concept of space or even this planet and its satellites, much less spacecraft or the old torus-station that was, in one way or another, her origin. Legends! Oh yes. She knew of the jann, and of Allah, of al-Bah'ram his name be blessed, and Malik-r—

"Al-Bah'ram?" He knew the name, or rather title. The over-wealthy crackpot and fanatic who had envisioned all this, and wrought it.

Oh yes. She knew of him. As they passed through a grove of dark, dark boles and tiny pink starshapes of blossoms and fungi in topaz and ruby and garnet, oyster and summer cloud, Johara told him what she knew of the Bah'ram.

It was nonsense.

He lived, though none had ever seen him. Of *course* not! He was beloved of Allah. All the world existed because of him. He had persuaded Allah to let him create this portion of Heaven and to people it with humans, in Allah's own image. Why? Why, for Allah's own pleasure. The mission of humankind was twofold: to be fruitful and multiply to fill His World, and to achieve perfection unto Allah. With a sigh she told Jimajin that her people had never succeeded in achieving perfection and suffered the Cooling for it; and that while she was of age and beyond, she had never been fruitful.

He ignored that last part, noting that their word for the Cooling, that evilly explained seasonal change, was Zamhar, which he assumed came from one of the names for the Muslim Cold Hell.

Myths. Legends. A benevolent, ever-watchful Bah'ram, eh, after a thousand years, watching over His People. Sure. He questioned her more.

Nor could he gain from her aught but that the Messenger of Allah and al-Bah'ram, King Dragon, did indeed exist. Yes, she had seen him. Yes, he spoke. No, *she* had not heard him. The Leader had; the *omda* of Kwait, and the Lionwoman, Her, the Speaker of Judgments. Of *course* others had seen him. No more than ten people in Kwait had *not* seen King Dragon!

So avowed Joharah of Kwait.

Superstition and myth. Legend and elephant excrement, the frustrated Allayth snarled—but his snarls were mental only.

They came to the brow of a long, long steep hill. Opposite and below their level, more forest stood darkly against a pearly sky, a sky of morning. The hill was grassed and strewn with rocks and outcrops of stone, with only a few scrubby trees hardly worthy of the name, all twisty and precariously perched. A fat green-and-blue rope of serpent lay on a ledge below, peacefully taking the sun like a carefree vacationer. A lizard scuttled in electric blue; far, far below a broad stream flowed smoothly, a handsome stripe of dark blue-green.

Allayth bade Johara remain near and squat at the edge of the long slope, and watch. He was discomfited a bit when she did not squat, but knelt close to his leg. He affected not to notice. He began to swing his symbol of bondage around and around his head until the chain no longer clinked but whirred. More and more loudly it keened, and then he released it.

Two meters of bronze links flew out and out, and farther still, tearing the air. He was inordinately proud when it fell into the surging water so far below.

"So much for slavery."

"Now mine," she said quietly.

"Yours is smaller and lighter and I want to keep it."

She looked up at him with huge soulful eyes surrounded by hair like cobwebbery done in jet. "You will enslave me with it? To you, Lion?"

He smiled. "No. It may be useful in another way. But tell me—who makes chain, Jo?"

"Hajars."

"It is made only in Hajarazad?"

"Yes. Kwait does not know how, and we—that is, Kwait—does not hunt people."

"Umm." So she had not conceived of other uses of chain. "And why do the Hajars take slaves?"

"No one knows. No one has been taken and returned. The Leader said that King Dragon will not tell him. We are not to know, then. Some think the Hajars eat people. Some think they make them hunt for them, or something. Some think the slaves are for King Dragon, and that is the reason he will not tell us. Besides, there has to be a good reason that al-Bah'ram and Malik-rukh allow Hajarazad and its people-hunters to exist."

"You think there's a good reason for everything, Johara?"

She sighed. "We all think that. We are supposed to think that." In a lower voice she added, "Some doubt."

That reminded him: "Oh—who is Sai?"

"The Tale-teller of Kwait, appointed by King Dragon himself. I saw him come one day, to land on the cliff above Kwait. We watched the Leader climb up to talk with him—hear his words, I mean. We saw King Dragon leap from the cliff and fly away, and the Leader came down to tell us that Sai had been chosen Tale-teller. He is . . . Sai was my friend. He thinks . . . differently." She jerked her head sharply up to look at him. "I have not lain with him."

He had not asked that, but he was male and gratified to hear the words.

"You needn't remain there kneeling, Jo—I just wanted you low while I disposed of the chain."

"I am comfortable here." She leaned lightly against his leg.

"Only Hajarazad makes chain. But jewelry is made in Kwait. Gauds."

"Oh, yes!" She held up an arm twice banded with big carven gauds, one of bronze and another of shell, set with bits of stone. Her earring-headdress rustled, not really jingling, when she shook her head sharply to make it move. "Oh yes. The best, Kwait makes. My boots I made myself, and decorated too."

"I love them, on you. And your necklace—"

"—Shells, from the river of Kwait."

"Beautiful. Who told Kwait how to make such beautiful gauds? This is art. Your earrings are spectacular." *I'd say their sale on Earth would support ten families*, he mused, and felt a little pang in his vitals. Earth. A place far away. Someplace he used to know. He'd not get back in time to publish in four years, or forty. "Your . . . your earrings," he repeated, picking up his train of thought with an effort. "They are works of art and skill both."

"Yes! *I* did not make these, I assure you! I have no such skill. But some have, and some do. King Dragon told us how. Told people of Kwait, I mean, long before I was born."

"Ah, ole Malik-rukh again. How long ago was this?"

She shrugged. "Generations. This bracelet my grandmother wore."

He sighed. Frustrations and frustrations! King Dragon and al-Bah'ram, over and over. Elephant excrement! "Ah . . . weapons. Smelting metals . . ."

"We have always had them, and the knowledge. King Dragon, of course, at the behest of al-Bah'ram be he blessed. Generations and generations ago. Kwait has always known."

King Dragon and the Bah'ram. A hyperglandular pterodactyl that talked and a sort of demigod-Mahomet figure. Never seen, of course. Personal friend and advisor to God and doubtless like this with Him. Sure. Allayth sighed again. He glanced down at the sunning snake: gone. Disturbed by the changing air currents of the whirling chain, he supposed. Ten or twelve meters below, the hillside abruptly extruded a waddling lizard in green and smoke, about a meter long on legs banded garishly with chartreuse. It looked this way and that, tasted the air with a tongue long as it was, and went waddling and sliding downhill. Above the forest on the far side of the stream, a pteranodon flew lazily, soaring as a sharp ugly outline against the pale sky. A dragon, but not King Dragon. It dived, vanished into the treetops.

"Johara . . . is there a tree that is soft, pithy, or a musseroun that must be cut with a knife?"

"Of course. Meatplant and pillowtop both. How can you not know these things?"

"Nine-point-nine-tenths of the things I know are of no value on—in your world, Johara. What I want is a target. I need to prac—"

"In my world. My lion—where have you come from?"

"Far and far and far again, Jo." He had a silly thought, one of those "Oh, you're from Europe; do you know—" things. "Have you ever seen anything strange fall from the sky?"

"Yes. Oh! Yes! Just after the Hajars took me, I saw something I could not explain. It did not seem to fall, but to come down, on stubby little wings that did not move. It seemed to be landing, like a dragon—but that was beyond trees, so I did not see it. It was shiny."

"Be damned. You're from America and you *do* know old Ahmet!"

"What?"

"I was in that thing you saw fall, Johara." Shaky ground, he told himself, but felt under compulsion to go on. "Its name is *Cygnet*. I came from—"

He waved a hand. "Up there. Out there. A monster of a bear attacked, and my pretty *Cygnet* was destroyed—slain. I only just escaped. Remember the fine boots I had, which Abdur took? No one of your world could make such boots."

"Or such a story," she said, and seemed on the point of laughter. Or of running.

"Have you ever heard of Earth, Johara?"

She sat away from his leg. "Yes! Of course."

His heart seemed to leap. "What do you know of Earth?"

Her eyes were big again. "What everyone knows. Do you not? Earth is the home of Iblees. It is where people go who have been evil and are dead."

He gazed down at her for a long while, and the miseries were on him. At last he swallowed, sighed, nodded. *Oh you bastard! O you rotten monster of a Bah'ram or whoever you are—how evilly you plotted, and how well–twistedly well–you planned! So Earth is the name of Hell, home of Eblis the Dark Lord of Death, is it? How lovely for possible "invaders" of "your" world, eh? What had he not thought of, the designer of this madhouse world of beauty and horror and death?*

"You are not now about to tell me that you are come from *there*, Lion Jim."

He shook his head sadly, sadly. "No, Joharah, of course not. No one could come from there." *Except that damned King Dragon and Bah'ram of yours!* "I am truly not of Ajjer, though, but one . . . uh, sent here."

"For . . . me?"

He smiled, though he didn't feel like smiling

just now. "No, not just for you, I mean." *I hope I
didn't come here to die for your salvation or the
Bah'ram's sins,* he thought. "Have—have you
heard of Terra, Johara?"

"Sometimes you call me Joharah," she said,
growling the terminal, "and sometimes merely
Johara. Never mind; I like it, al-Layth. Tara. No.
No one has heard of Tara."

"You are a Kwaiti."

"Yes." The clouds came onto her face. "I was
. . ."

"I am a Terri. I am from Terra, Jo, my lioness."

"And . . ." She was striving to assimilate it, he
saw, whether she could ever understand it or
not—or even, really, accept it. "And now . . .
your Signet is destroyed. You cannot return to
Tara?"

She saw the pain in his eyes before he turned
away, and she rose in an undulant movement of
sinuousness he would have enjoyed watching.
She pressed to him. He felt the movements of her
jaw as she spoke, her face against his back.
Her hands were very warm, on him.

"Did Jim al-Layth have a woman, in his world of
Tara?"

"Once," he said to the air and the incredible
blue sky of the hellish planet called Heaven.
"Once, on Terra, I had a woman."

She pressed him strongly. He was impressed
with her strength, by it. "Once, in Kwait, I had a
man. We were wed, and in two days only he went
forth on the hunt, and a bumblecow slew him."

He heard and could not forget his own problems, but he heard hers and swerved to it. "O,
Joharah. I am sorry."

"I am sorry no longer, for me. I am sorry for you, my lion. I would have been a slave to horror: Raafar. Then I was slave to Hajarazad's people-hunters. A lion came, a sad strong lion, and he made me free. I am sad only because he is sad."

He put his hands onto her hands on him, then, and drew them from him so that he could turn. He held her for a long, long while, and when they sank down it was in tenderness and mutual need.

16

Year 113: The riot of the Blues in the main rec
area today was ended by the *Actual Appearance* of Al-Bah'ram! No one had ever seen
Him before; no one! I was shocked and ele-
vated by his appearance. We all were, and
some fell to their knees. Those burning eyes
beneath the black turban—the Spokesman of
God! He seems no more than forty years of
age.
. . . Known Blues numbered 27. Today our
numbers are fewer by 33. We are safe again.
All praise to God's Spokesman! Still, Hussayn
and I look forward to raising a child on a real
planet, under a real sky and sun, fearsome as
that concept is . . .

—863 Ashrif

"A long time ago, I asked a question. About a
target for arrows."

"I remember. I am sorry that I interrupted."

"No you're not, and I'm not either. Interrupted
and disrupted, and I'll thank you to do it again,
too. And, I still need that target. I need to practice
with this bow, and I want to be able to retrieve the
arrows."

"Oh. You are not good with the bow?"

"It is not mine," he temporized. "Or wasn't. These are not my arrows. We need to know each other, my new bow and arrows."

"Yes." She sat up, jiggling, and he squeezed his eyes shut and looked away.

"Do cover yourself," he said, and rolled over to do that for himself.

"You have no liking for me naked?"

"You know very and very well that I have, woman. I just think it best if I am not distracted again. Right now, I mean."

"All right. Come."

They walked from the cliff's edge and reentered the forest. After a short meander, she pointed to a fungus some three meters tall. Its stipe was as thick as she. Even in the gloom of thick verdure, he could see that the yellow-white cap was very large indeed.

"Pillowtop," Johara said. "It is not good to eat, but its head makes a nice cushion and does not decay for many hours. The stem has to be cut."

It did. He used the pre-sword, whose total length was not as long as his arm from pit to fingertips. Sixty centimeters, perhaps. About forty-five of them composed the blade. He had to chop eight times, though with more skill he might have felled the fungus in five. The hard part was hitting the same place twice. Part of the cap broke on impact with a chittapel's bole and then the ground. Lying on that break-flattened portion of its perimeter, the puffy, only slightly convex cap now stood higher than his waist.

He wrestled its considerable weight into position so that it was behind and between two trees.

The diameter of one was greater than his height. That should save his wild shots, provided they went a bit rightward.

He stepped well away and put three arrows into the fungus cap and one into the smaller tree, and backed several paces, and put another into the same tree and then two more into the fungus. And another, high and almost missing. The ninth arrow zoomed between the trees well above the target. It vanished among the ferny bushes that thrust up there in restless clumps.

"A bad arrow," he said, impressed with the bow and himself. "Glad I learned that with a target. If I had relied on that one, we could have died."

"You are good with the bow and so it was certainly a bad arrow." She seemed bored. "How many more are there?"

"Only four." He avoided mentioning that the bad arrow was the one he had taken from Hussayn's throat. "Can we eat the target, then?"

"Oh no. It is not poison, but it ferments inside the stomach and the gas is painful and loud. Also, it stinks."

A straightforward answer, he thought, if more than adequate. And he zinged the other four arrows into the target, two going high but taking the fungal cap anyhow. That felt good. He could handle a bow, all right.

"Well, I'm sorry we can't eat it," he said as he paced to it, beaming. "I'm hungry. Aren't you?"

"The hunger of a lion is as fearsome a thing as thunderstorm," she said, in what he took to be a quotation. "You could easily shoot us a lizard on the hillside, while I gather the best musserouns. Are you fond of leeks?"

"Not today, please. I am not going to eat lizard today, either. Oh damn."

Two arrows had gone completely through the target. The bushes beyond were clumpily thick and viciously thorny. He found only one of the shafts, and that cost him several scratches. A third arrow was broken. Split, Robin Hood fashion, by another. He did not compliment himself on such marksmanship that wasted a valuable shaft. He should have thought of that. He did save that arrowhead, and with her shorter knife dug out those he had imbedded in the tree. He marked them, to remind himself that they might be untrustworthy.

"The bow tends to the left—or I do—and might tend to loft a bit. Best aim is slightly rightward, and low." He was talking to himself, while she moved as busily about, choosing edible fungi and muttering that she saw no meatplant. She tugged up a couple of tubers and asked for the knife to go after a larger one. He tossed it over and took stock while he returned the arrows to his quiver.

Mighty hunter Allayth. Nine good arrows and two questionable ones. And someone else's wooden bow strung with I-don't-want-to-know-what. A sixty-centimeter-long pre-sword that is definitely and unaccountably iron, and a leopard-hide(?) loincloth and Balzac. And a loyal woman. Together we have killed a man but flee another who is big as a bear but surely isn't even following.

My God! Killed a man! All that blood! Old Abdulassan. Why I remember when that puffball let go and he . . . all that blood . . .

Vomit gushed from him and he dropped to his

knees to let it pour forth. His body heaved until it hurt and his stomach was trying to crowd into his mouth. She came to him in the manner of a soothing mother, patting his lurching back and crooning, fortunately not knowing the reason for the lion's sudden illness. Jimajin the Lion. Archer and mighty hunter.

She continued to comfort him, patting and crooning and pressing close to his back, until he was altogether over it and feeling something entirely different from disgust and sickness. Again. But when he turned amorously to her, he saw in an instant that his sour vomitous breath was disgusting to her, and so he swallowed hard and sublimated.

Many kilometers away, more than two dozen dragons, their rudimentary "brains" linked to King Dragon because their Creator had so planned and arranged it, lofted and began flapping out in coveys. Their mission, dimly perceived in heads nigh devoid of brainstuff and yet perceived, was to find those Raafar also sought. The Eyes—King Dragon—had found sure evidence that not one but two had come here in the destroyed little ship from Earth(?), and that one of them had left the scene under his own power. Nor had any corpse been found.

And the readout marked ABDUR had gone blank and cold.

17

Year 113: All tapes were this day erased by order of Allah and His Spokesman, Al-Bah'ram. 871 Noureddeen slew himself today. The maintenance of private journals has been forbidden by Allah and al-Bah'ram, His name be blessed.

 —1 Sulayman, Captain, for Al-Bah'ram
Year 114: There were no entries past the 113th year of Station Jauhar.

"The feel of life was keen because the sense of death was near," a man named Charles Lindbergh had once written. Jimajin Allayth, moving through the forest of Ajjer, feeling un-leonine with his lioness at his side, knew what that sad once-hero had meant. Death was a silent third companion.

The best tracker in the world was most likely on their trail, or seeking it. A pterosaur had tried to attack them or so they assumed; a tree had got in the way and the monster had flapped away with the noise of a leather-sailed ship in a good wind. A skink-like Thing as long as Johara's height had challenged them while they were at pause to cut and sharpen a spear. It would have done more

than challenge, too, had the mighty hunter not
sent an arrow at it. Somehow the shaft went directly into one chartreuse eye, and the lizard
floundered noisily away. Later Allayth discovered that the arrow had been one of those he had
pried out of the tree.

*So damned scared I didn't even choose one of
the arrows I knew was good,* he thought, flogging
himself from habit. *We could have been killed!
Mighty hunter is a dummy!*

The feel of life was keen in him, all right, and he
was grateful for that life.

The point eluded him. The point was that he
had drawn an arrow, nocked it, pulled the bow,
sighted, and removed the menace by shooting it
in one cup-sized eye. All under stress, at a dozen
paces. That occurred to him only an hour later,
and eased his self-castigation. Yet he still thought
of himself as "Mighty Hunter" only in a satirical
way. He could not quite believe the truth: to Johara, he was manifestly a mighty hunter and protector. She had forgotten depression; he did not
realize that he was now seeking the miseries,
merely from habit.

Perhaps fleeing Raafar and definitely maintain-
ing a westward course, they skirted prickly furzy
growths and giant fungi and more gigantic trees
and vermiform tangles of vine. Through the
canopying trees he spotted the nearest moon
again.

It occurred to him that while this one was visible even during the day—if one happened to be
able to see the sky for the treetops, and happened
to be looking—he had never seen either of the
others. One of course would be a mere point of

light without discernible disc, visible only at
night and indistinguishable from a star. The middle moon . . . well, it would be recognizable as
a satellite, if one happened to see it at night. It was
too small and far to be visible in daylight.

They called the nearest one "Baydr," which
was simply the Old Arabic word for "full moon."
It was also called Shirzad: "Lion-born." He didn't
know why.

Next it occurred to him that one could measure
time on Ajjer, in less than unwieldy increments of
seventy or so hours; the period of daylight. He
reflected on that as they walked; Johara was no
loquacious companion. He knew very well that
Baydr/Shirzad went 'round in five and a quarter
hours. With a bit of time to observe and a bit of
observing, followed by the setting of a mental
clock (or implementation of instinct or "instinct"), he should be able to work out the length
of an hour, and work from that. Shirzad was never
visible, after all, for more than three hours.

Why? What did it matter?

*Because, damn it, I'm accustomed to it. On
Earth and in space, my kind has always measured
time, and I am accustomed to that. It makes us
feel . . . comfortable. Knowing what time it is,* he
mused, screwing up his face as they slushed
through a wide stenchy area of decaying fungus,
*makes a person feel in control. God knows I need
that illusion now, when I have about as much
control over environment and destiny as a
paramecium!*

They emerged from the forest quite suddenly,
and very nearly went right over the cliff.

That was how they had learned that for hours

they had been atop a broad mesa. Hours after leaving the other long long incline, they stood at the brink of another. This time they looked down a far steeper and rockier slope, at what might have been the same river they had seen a wake-period and a sleep and two couplings ago.

Charming. Down that ugly scarp and across a river at the edge of another forest, they watched a (modified) allosaurus tangle with a Something: an erect saurian beasty that was not quite up to King Lizard status. That was T. Rex.

The two mindless horrors were busily destroying fernstipes and leaves, fungi, lichen, blossoms, turf, smaller trees and each other, all amid enough noise to herald the topple of Jericho's walls. At a cautiously chosen distance two hyænodons patiently sat, doglike on their haunches. Watching. Waiting. One of the combatants would presumably be slain and, with luck, not totally consumed. Or perhaps the victor would be sufficiently weakened to be pulled down.

"Is everything here inimical? Is that all there is?" Allayth was crying out to a seeming universe gone less than just unfriendly. "Fights, attacks, warnings, fear, murder? Blood and rivalry and mistrust and blood and scavengers? God, what have I done, coming here? Where am I?!"

She looked at him with concerned woman's eyes and saw a large boy close onto despair. Her hand came onto his wrist, and he jerked in surprise. "See the kalbodons?"

He blinked. *Kalbodons*, yet! A completely bastard combination of two languages: *kalb/qelb* was old Arabic for the Terrali word *dawg*, which was *dwahg* in some areas of Earth. He nodded. Yes, he

EBREBAN MAROTO

saw the "dog-toothed ones:" the hyænodons. Almost-dogs; almost-wolves.

"Yes."

"Once when I was just a girl I left Kwait and went awalking and went to sleep. That was stupid. I could have died. All of us want to eat and I might have been something's dinner."

He heard the difference, the philosophy of one who was native to Ajjer, and he blinked as he gazed at her. "Yes," he said, for want of anything better to say, and to elicit more, to hear her story.

"When I woke up a kalbodon was standing closer than the length of my arm and it was looking at me with pale, pale eyes. I was scared enough to die. I am between His hands, I thought, and lay where I was. Afraid to move! It stood there and we stared at each other. It did not growl and I did not know what to do. After a long time I realized that it didn't either. I had not moved and one of my arms needed to, badly. After a while I remember I thought that he might need to move, too. Then I wondered if he too might be afraid to move. Perhaps he had not scented me but had just come upon me by accident, and just froze; and then I woke up."

Allayth wanted to ask how old she had been, and he didn't. It was the most she had spoken at one time, in his presence.

"My arm was starting to hurt and I knew I had to do something. I was just a girl. I spoke. I said, 'Hello kalbodon, kalyliyya. You have pretty eyes. I wish I had such pretty eyes. Are your legs not starting to hurt?'" Johara shook her head at the sound of her long-ago words. She smiled softly, in reminiscence. "Its ears jumped up and it backed,

one step. Three paws back, one still forward.
Poised, like a child before a race. So I moved too; I
moved my hand, just a little. It looked at my hand
with its ears straight up, a little forward. If I had
been older, I would have been afraid to wiggle my
fingers while it was staring at them. I did it, then.
Almost at the same time that kalbodon sat, just
lowered its rump and then stretched out on its
belly. It looked at me with those strange eyes like
the palms of my hands and I remember thinking
that if it could talk, it would.''

She turned to gaze away from him. The vista ran
forever, treetops merging into a green sea that
became gray-blue and then purplish as they went
bravely to meet the horizon. He looked down the
rocky slope and across the river. The allosaur had
won; the almost-tyrannosaurus had quit the field.
The (almost) allosaurus went back to eating trees.
The hyaenodons followed Prince Lizard.

"What happened then?"

"I said some more things to it," Johara said,
almost murmuring now, "and it put its head
down on its paws and stared at me so that it
looked childlike, looking up from under brows.
Expectant? Something like that. Very slowly, I
stood up. It looked nervous and made a whining
noise. I backed and backed and then I turned and
went back to Kwait. I did not run. I heard it, just
faintly. It followed me right up to Kwait.''

"Followed you!"

"Yes. Just . . . just followed. The same as when
I was asleep; as if it just wanted to be with me. It
followed me right up to Kwait, and Hajjan yelled
and threw his spear right into the kalbodon. My
kalbodon. I wondered if it might have stayed with

me. They ate it. I would not eat any."

He slid an arm across her back to her far shoulder and squeezed her to him. Her hair tickled his arm and that was fine. Then he sat down, thinking. Aloud.

"A carnivore. It affrighted you, but it meant you no harm. A hunting carnivore. Maybe it is instinct, with dogs and even pre-dogs. I see, I see, Johara. Not all non-humanlife on Ajjer is unfriendly, then. Nor—I hope—is all human life."

"Of *course* not!"

"It's the only kind I have seen, Johara."

"No!" Her eyes were huge, anxious to change his mental set. "No—you have seen me!"

He held her close, awkwardly while they sat on the ground. "Yes. Oh yes, Jo. Oh yes. I've seen you."

He sat and held her and stared at nothing until she pulled away, gently.

"We . . . we have to keep moving . . ."

"Yes."

They paced along the precipice until they found a place that would allow their descent with a minimum of danger. A few meters below, a ledge ran along the rocky face of the scarp like one of those flat-topped, spongy-looking lichens that grew horizontally on trees. Onto that he dropped the headless spear, holding his breath until he saw it would not roll off. The ledge was long, wrapping around the hill, but hardly wide. They started down. The allosaurus, grazing, was moving on. Allayth assumed that it would be gone by the time they reached bottom.

Then what? That was no stream; it was a real river. He tried to think of a way to cross. Tried to decide which way to walk along the bank, once they reached it. And he descended, scraping thighs and a knee, hurting a forearm and a fingertip. Jim the Lion, in a skimpy leopard skin. A stone fled clattering away under his foot and he was very still for a long long minute, choking his heart back down. Then he resumed his descent.

They were on the ledge when they heard the noise and looked up to see the five pterosaurs.

I didn't know they came in coveys, he later remembered thinking, and then one of those hideous big flying lizards sort of tilted and peeled off from the others and came straight at him.

It was crazy. Every bit of it, every minute of it was crazy. In the first place he moved as he had against the big skink: instantly, rather than going all shaky-stiff with fear. In the second, he used the spear not as a spear but as an oversized club, a quarterstaff. It was too heavy and thick for that and he used it so just the same. With a two meter pole of hard green wood he stood on the ledge less than half that width, and he bashed the attacking bird-lizard right in the beak.

The thing was unwieldy and ungainly. His blow knocked it sidewise and it never did catch itself, but fell flopping and bouncing and scrawking all the way down and down until it bounced off a nasty rearing pile of rocks at the base of the scarp and splashed into the river. It kept flopping as it was borne downstream, unable to take off from the water.

"Get the chain from around my waist!" he yelled, because another one was coming at them. She took the spear instead and braced it for the flying monster to impale himself. It veered off and went up on leathery wings, each big as Dracula's cloak.

He pulled her former chain of slavery off himself and used it to flail at the third dragon, coming in from the side. The chain connected and had he not let go he'd have gone down with the attacker. With the chain across one eye and around its neck, it fell scrawking hideously as a whole army of jays, sliding sidewise on air for a dekameter before it caught itself on wildly flapping wings. It soared away, not back, with the chain flashing. It was losing altitude steadily, but Allayth and Johara were too busy to exult.

A fourth pterodactyl attacked at the same time as the second returned in anger. One from above and leftish; the other almost directly above, starting a dive. The chain was gone and Johara had the spear/quarterstaff. With sweat rolling off him, necessity reminded Allayth of his bow.

The dragon dived and she braced the long sharpened sapling again and Allayth dragged the strung bow off his back and the other attacker came sweeping in from the side and high and Allayth had the bow in his right hand so he kept it there while he snapped an arrow into place and the oncoming ptero opened wide its long long beak to show long thin tongue and viciously pointed teeth and it emitted a ghastly horrible hideous screech and the arrow went straight in and through its tongue and down the dragon's throat while Allayth dived sidewise because it was still rushing down at him.

He very nearly went off the ledge. Clinging with both hands, he tried to dig in his toes as well.

The creature's awful cry broke off into some-

thing as hideous: all bubbly now, with the blood
that gushed up and out as it slammed into the
rocky wall almost directly above him. Flapping
and flopping, it fell backward. Allayth felt the
cool spray of blood on his legs and a wing dragged
across him. The claws missed. The outsized
rhamphorhynchus went down and down to hit
the same jumble of stone as its fellow. This one
did not bounce. It splattered all over the jagged
rock. The saurian body writhed eel-like while the
wings moved only in spasms.

It was a long way down and Allayth's head
hung over the edge of the shelf. He clung with
both hands, squeezed both eyes shut, and backed
from the edge.

He twisted his head around in time to see that
Johara's attacker had again veered from the thick
stake she had braced for it. This time she rammed

the wrist-thick spear up into its pale belly. The
point went in and in, and for a moment her feet
left the ledge. Allayth cried out. The buffeting of
enormous wings knocked her to her knees, while
the spear remained in the winged saurian. The
spitted dragon went bounce-flopping down and
down and down.

Neither of them had time to consider that they
were hardly scratched and had accounted for four
of the horrors prosaically named "wing fingers."
Everything had happened very very rapidly; too
rapidly even for fear; the desperate need for action
had ruled. Had breathing been a voluntary act
they both would surely have smothered.

At least it's over, he thought, *and I can lie here
and pant for a week . . .*

The remaining dragon was hovering. Allayth
assumed it was fearful in view of the mayhem
done on the rest of the squadron. Then he saw that
it was awaiting reinforcements, and reinforce-
ment was on the way. Here came one of the devils
flying back, a gargoyle shape against the sky.
Judging from the messy aspect of one of its eyes, it
was the dragon Allayth had lashed with the chain.
It must have succeeded in dragging the links off
on a tree across the river.

A thought fleeted across his mind: these things
surely could not think. Therefore this concerted
action tended to indicate . . . intelligent direction?

Then Johara's voice got through to him.

"Al-layth! Jeemajeen! My lion, my lion!
Hurry—a cave!"

No questions asked. He snatched up his bow
while he rose. He raced to where she was vanish-

ing into the face of the hillside, just where the ledge vanished around the strong incline. The mouth of the cave was hardly large and in his haste he scraped himself as he hurled himself inside. He did not care. There seemed adequate space within the hillside hollow, which was also pleasantly cool. Drawing the long-knife that had been Abdulassan's, he let go the bow lest he forget and break the valuable weapon by using it as a club. Even as he swung back to the opening, he felt the wind of the pterosaur's wings.

The rhamphorhynchus was holding itself aloft just outside, the ledge not quite wide enough for it to light. When it darted its head within, Allayth struck. The blade slid off the long ugly beak, which was withdrawn. Immediately the second dragon was there, repeating the other's behavior. Allayth let himself sprawl and roll onto his back. He struck upward, to slice leathery saurian hide just behind the base of the beak. Blood spurted and that one, too, withdrew.

The first one returned and he chopped. The champing of the beak missed, but its long hard bulk knocked him against the rocky wall, hard. He cursed, beat away beak and teeth, lost his head, followed the withdrawing beak, and slashed the creature under its throat as it started its upward flapping. Downbeating wings knocked him down and more eerily lukewarm blood splashed him.

Badly wounded, the panicky dragon plunged. It struck no rocks, for its wings were working to some extent and an air current must have helped. Dropping almost straight down toward the water, it caught itself with hard-working wings at the last instant, and crashed into a couple of mighty trees on the other side of the river. The thing kept flopping about while it bled to death.

Allayth, panting, saw the other dragon flop-flapping away. It was making headway despite its wound.

"Five of them," he muttered, looking around for something to wipe his blade and himself. There was nothing. Only stone and more of it. And more blood.

Five of them. Four downed and presumed dead. One in retreat, wounded. God and stars! I did —we did it! Five . . . a concerted attack. The last one waited carefully for the other one to come back, too, so they could attack together. Is that pterodactyl behavior? (Finding a monograph on pterodactylian behavior was far more difficult than being independent, on Earth—or finding treatises, learned and otherwise, on unicorns.) *These are a lot bigger than the rhamphorhynchus or archaeopteryx that once flew on Earth, right up into the Cretaceous era. Was the brainpower of these heightened with their size? Were they genengineered with cooperative behavior, wolfpack attacks?*

Or were they . . . sent? Directed, guided, controlled? If that's possible, then by whom? "King Dragon?" *But if there is a King Dragon . . . who guides him or it?*

A hand slid onto his shoulder, and the most romantic of writers would have been hard put to call it soft and delicate. "My lion? How are you hurt?"

"Scratches . . . bruises. That's all. And none of the scratches are from claws—Jo? Are you all right?" He twisted around in concern.

"Yes. Oh yes. Come. Come into the cave."

"Yuh. I could use the feeling of a haven, about now. I could use . . ."

They went into the cave, and proved the existence of an enigma, if not its exact cause. It was old knowledge that speeded heartbeat and breathing accompanied by adrenaline rush were characteristics of both anxiety and lustful desire. Was fearful anxiety the long-sought aphrodisiac? Hardly; both sexes had long experienced the opposite. But in the face of deadly anger—and after its removal—humans sought relief in each other. Because there was something to prove? Was it genetic? Was a man about to go into combat or other deadly danger genetically programmed to try to father his own replacement, the ancient mandate, in the event of his death? And afterward . . . perhaps the strong intimations of mortality just experienced spurred both sexes in the same way. Perhaps. Perhaps it was as simple as strong psychological relief suggesting and leading to physical relief.

Not all problems and enigmas were solved, on Earth. Johara and Jimajin did not solve this one on Ajjer. They did prove its strong call and interplanetary existence, and tension went away.

18

Johara slid into a smiling sleep. Allayth did not. His mind continued uncontrollably active, seeking.

An organized attack. Intelligence directed? Yes! What about the source of that direction? What brain? It was not likely that it was within the little reptilian, pre-avian heads of the attackers. Therefore . . .

All right, he thought. *Let's say there is a King Dragon. Suppose he's out there right now, flapping and sliding around in the air, observing this cave he knows he can't get into. And . . . reporting back? Is he intelligent? Is he a construct, with a person inside?* Not likely—but the thing might well represent a man just as Johara had said: Messenger of al-Bah'ram. And "personal" representative, that is, a spy set long ago to watch over the planet. A mobile scanner, and still operating, reporting to . . . no one? Maybe. A bionic construct, modified both biologically (genetically-cellularly) and mechanically; cybernetically?

Someone wants us dead. It may be a centuries-old construct, carrying out a programmed set of instructions. It may be someone living; there is technology somewhere on this world. At least

there is some machinery. So—assuming a living person or persons unknown, that someone wants us dead and sent the dragons. Pterodactyls so big they are dragons.

Why? Because someone knows who I am—or rather, knows my off-planet origin? The over-lord(s) whose presence Cygnet's scanners reported . . . while theirs reported our presence? Ah . . . !

We coped. We handled their attack. Did we exhibit extra-Ajjeri intelligence/ability? I doubt that. But they will try again . . . if all this surmising is close to the mark. What do we do about it, then? If he/it is flying around out there right now . . . what do we do?

What do we do?

We? I didn't decide to jump Musa; that was reflex. I didn't decide to jump Abdulassan, either. Johara and Hussayn did. I had no choice but to flee Raafar, or felt I hadn't; call that Johara's "decision," with me going along. Once we were out of his sight, I decided to stop and get the chains off. Johara wanted to go on. We went on. When I decided to stop and take them off a while later, we didn't, because she didn't want to. We crossed the stream. She decided we shouldn't leave the chains for Raafar to find, so we carried the damned heavy things for kilometers and kilometers. "We should have a spear," Johara said, and then, when she wanted to stop, we stopped. We cut the spear and my finger. It was she who found this cave, too.

Before that, I did what Cicada wanted—and that brought disaster. Never mind that if the bear had come while we were in the ship and if he had pushed it over, we would both be dead. She de-

cided. I didn't, except when she forced me—the hard decisions. Then the bear and the pre-dogs decided things for me, and after that Abdur and company did.

I haven't made a single decision on this planet!—except to head west, west. Not one! What a total simpering namby-pamby dud . . .

And yet . . . and yet by Allah, sir, you have proven yourself a coper! You taught Musa respect. You took out Abdulassan. That skink-thing, too! The dragons! and Jo came, too!

He sat staring at nothing, thinking, eyes wide. I never knew. I must be what is called a coper, the same as Johara is: one who copes. More, I am pretty obviously a man of action—something I never would have known on Earth! God and stars—I'm even competent!

Elated, he dwelt on that, on his actions. Analyzing. The spear he had not handled so well; he had forgotten or ignored its point and used it as a club. Stick with the bow, he told himself. And . . . fists! That was certainly effective against poor silly dead Musa . . . and it taught some respect to Abdur and his Hajarazadi bravos, too. And with something in his fists . . .

Johara was awakened by harsh grating sounds: the simultaneous whetting of a dagger and a long-knife on the stone wall of the cave. Frowning, impressed by his astonishing ability to use both hands at once, she turned away to think about him while she worked at cleansing herself and her clothing of blood that was not hers. She enjoyed thinking about him, and her, and had already decided that it was best not to question much. Johara's experience had taught her never to hope too much.

He discovered her so, when he decided he had labored long enough at repairing and improving edge and point of two iron weapons. He moved to her and gently rubbed her back and neck. Thinking, feeling. Could this stone/bronze/iron(?) age woman be the woman for him, the women who—

Best not to think too much about that. Right now, neither of them had any options at all. Each was the only store in town. It was a mighty big town, some 39,000 kilometers in circumference . . . how far to the nearest emissions center?

"Ummm . . . that feels so nice . . ."

Thus supported and encouraged, he continued rubbing and kneading her back, neck and shoulders, with occasional little excursions up forward. New thoughts and whole new concepts and possibilities toyed with his brain—and the lethery *slap, slap* sounds made him turn.

His hands remained on Johara, frozen into im-

mobility. For a long, long moment he stared at a draconic head just outside the cave mouth. The head was at least a third again as large as those of the outsize pterosaurs they had fought an hour ago. Stared into big glassy-glittery yellow eyes surmounted by a weird crest or horn . . .

Then King Dragon flapped hard, and rose straight up. Allayth watched the rise of a long, long, *long* tail.

"Excuse me," he muttered inanely, heart starting to pound, and he took his hands from her to reach for bow and quiver.

By the time she had turned, he had an arrow nocked to the string and was at the cave's mouth. "Come and get it!" he yelled, and Johara sprawled forward to see what—

"No!"

King Dragon wheeled in air and came back, flapping hard then soaring, racing in, diving, while Allayth drew, sighted, took a deep breath, held and King Dragon screamed, came whistling in at twenty or more kilometers an hour while Allayth opened the fingers of his left hand and pounced sidewise.

With the arrow standing out of its head between its eyes just left of center, Malik-rukh slammed into the rocky face of the scarp. From two meters' distance Allayth loosed another arrow—and missed.

King dragon clawed at the ledge, tottered, wheeled as it fought for balance, failed to find it. It fell off the rock shelf even as Allayth loosed a third arrow. More by luck than skill, it transpierced the tail of the impossibly huge lizard. The first man ever to attack King Dragon pounced to the edge of the shelf to look down. He was disappointed. King Dragon struck neither rocks nor water. It slammed both wings down hard, lifted, and soared up above the trees across the river.

Wheeling, it came back.

Allayth nocked a fourth arrow and glanced at Johara.

"Get back."

"You—you cannot shoot Malik rukh!"

"I have. King Dragon first tried to kill me. He bears no messages to us, just death. He sent the lesser ones to kill us and when they failed, the king came. Get back, and hush!"

King Dragon stayed high. It cleared the ledge by meters and the top of the scarp by then. Allayth waited. After several minutes he thrust his arrow back into the quiver and unstrung his bow without pausing to think how easy and natural these actions were for him. Johara saw the smooth play and bunching of excellent muscles.

"Be damned. The son-of-a-bitch isn't coming back. Jo . . . would you mind just holding the questions and giving me a nice back rub? I need it, and I have some thinking to do."

She was in semi-shock. King Dragon had attacked, been wounded, fled. King Dragon was a part of life, of superstition, religion. "Yes . . . all . . . all right," she told Lord Jimajin the Mighty.

"Ahhh," he sighed, and let himself sag, brain and body. Soon he had coaxed himself into the necrolaxed state he had learned was optimum for best use of his (almost) total recall. Johara rubbed and kneaded, trembling a little.

Once again he considered the tapes he and Cicada had viewed and listened to. The records of the private and even surreptitious thoughts of people dead nine hundred hears, along with Station Jauhar; the Mausoleum . . .

Year 37: *Al-Bah'ram spoke today . . . voice is so strong, so commanding. So it was in my father's time!*

Year 73: *The Bah'ram made the announcement in his strong, strong voice. It does so inspire confidence. It could be the voice of Mahomet, returned . . .* Year 80: *I must not doubt, or let anyone know. I command in his name—His name, one is tempted to say, vocally capitalizing—and though I have heard his strong, commanding voice that so inspires confidence, I have never seen him. I! It is incredible; the Bah'ram must by now be a hundred years old . . .* Year 83: *. . . attempt . . . on the Command Quarters, He spoke to us all. All-Bah'ram himself! How strong his voice, emanating from every speaker. . . . How we should love to see him! Yet all understand . . . the necessity for his remaining apart from us, above us. How commanding, how inspiring that voice and his words! He is eternal. He watches over us and keeps us. Glory to Allah and al-Bah'ram!*

Strong, strong voice . . . inspires confidence . . . never seen him . . . a hundred years old . . . never seen him . . . apart from us, above us . . . voice . . . Glory to al-Bah'ram . . .

Year 93: *. . . women actually supposed themselves equal; how majestic of Allah and al-Bah'ram not to destroy them for their temerity . . .* (814 Sareed) Year 94: *I have heard other tapes, though it is illicit and forbidden. It is not possible . . . that of which none dares speak: al-Bah'ram's longevity. . . . The man must have cloned himself . . .* (814 Sareed) Same year: *I cannot curb this quest for knowledge, knowledge.*

It affects me as an infection. It is a fever, a flame in my blood. I can hardly live with myself for wanting to know more, more. Has he kept a log? (814 Sareed) *Same year: It has been five sleeps now since anyone has seen 814 Sareed. . . . Queries filed to the Leader have not been answered. . . . Sareed was driven by . . . evil thirst for knowledge. Al-Bah'ram has told us that there are things we are not to know. Why can some not accept this?*

A hundred years old . . . voice . . . never seen him . . . Woman's place in al-Islam . . . must have cloned himself, and more than once . . . illicit forbidden/evil thirst for knowledge/there are things we are not to know . . .

Year 100: Today Our Bah'ram addressed us all through every speaker in every sector. I was enthralled! The words of the Leader! . . . his voice, tones made me nervous . . . Who am I to judge God's spokesman; Creator of a Planet and Leader of us All. He says Jauhar is not ready for us and we are not ready for Jauhar. Enthralled . . . voice made me nervous . . . not ready for Jauhar Not ready for Jauhar . . . (Jamsheed, Blue!) *(Same year) I have petitioned Him again and again, and this time my wording was strong, and I sent it around the Captain, His damned appointed Warden!* (Jamsheed, BLUE!) *(Same year) Everyone is wondering what has become of Jamsheed. . . . Some of us are beginning to wonder, and talk. Yet we must do so in secret . . .*

Year 113: The riot of the Blues . . . was ended today by the Actual Apppearance of Al-Bah'ram! . . . some fell to their knees . . . the Spokesman of God! He seems no more than forty years of age. . . . We are safe again. All praise to God's

*Spokesman! Still . . . (Same year) All tapes were
this day erased by order of Allah and His
Spokesman, Al-Bah'ram. 871 Noureddeen slew
himself today. The maintenance of private journals has been forbidden by Allah and His
Spokesman, Al-Bah'ram.—1 Sulayman, Captain,
for Al-Bah'ram.*

Year 114: No entries. There were no entries past
Year 113.

Allayth's eyes snapped open to stare at nothing.

Had all tapes, private and personal as well as
Ship's Records, been destroyed, we wouldn't
have found anything. Therefore they were not.
People keep them illicitly. There were none after
the 113th year. Therefore there were no people
left to keep journals. The Blues must have been a
rebel group. They shook the tyrant, and 33 people
died that day, though the Blues numbered fewer.
They shook him, and he—He—showed himself,
capitalized and all. About forty years old.
Hardly—more like 260! He was 141 when they left
Earth . . . and back then life expectancy was 173:
Max. Looked about forty. More and more totali-
tarian. Al-Islam, old style, with women returned
to a status lower than an ant's belly. More and
more repression, intolerance of any sort of questions or dissent: megalomania!

The existence of the Blues and their revolt
shook him, Allayth thought, staring at nothing.
He was suspicious of everyone, everyone and
everything, every question. He couldn't stand it.
Nor could they. He suspected or learned that they
were disobedient, still keeping journals. Maybe
women refused veils. . . .

Cloned himself! Of course! And in the 113th
year he cracked. Jauhar-al-Ajr was ready and more

than ready, and the people of Station Jauhar were not. So . . . God's Own Spokesman murdered every last one of them, and the station, and brought his self-contained Command Quarters—a whole section of a torus-ship!—down here. Set down over in the west somewhere. How many fetuses might he have had; how many clones of others on the ship; how many children who would forget?

He must have had himself confused with God by that time. He taught them how to dig ores and smelt. *Gave* them Fire, no doubt. Laid out the Laws, according to Allah and "al-Bah'ram, his name be blessed!" And they multiplied. spread out. He grandly gave them the great gift of jewelry-making—or maybe permission to make what people naturlly think of: personal decoration. Ah, Great Spokesman for Allah; God's Advisor and Best Friend, no doubt!

And then he had to . . . to keep tabs.

To see that they obeyed the Law: *His* Law, So—he re-modified one of his giant pterosaurians, or an unused egg. Perhaps added a bit of technology, too? Does King Dragon have a cybernetic larynx and heat-sensing apparati and scanners for eyes? His Messenger! His . . . spy. That way he kept all knowledge from them; any sort of vehicle would have set them wondering, would have given them some knowledge. But a giant among giant pterodactyls . . . that was his vehicle! Not only was it not suspect, it enhanced things for him; an object of superstittion and awe. Malik-rukh!

Allahuma! All these people, held down under a harsher foot than that of the Church of Rome from A.D. 400 or so right up to the end of the twentieth

century! All the dead Ajjeri . . . Allahuma! What
a monster, this ancient, fanatic, cracked
megalomaniac called al-Bah'ram! *Kahna!*
Enough!

Cygnet may have picked up evidence of his
installation—while its scanners picked up *Cygnet.* Maybe the *nth* clone of al-Bah'ram still lives
and maybe it doesn't. Maybe the equipment still
operates—as King Dragon does. It found *Cygnet.*
It must have found evidence of me, and knows
that I escaped. One man . . . and God does not
welcome an intelligent interloper in *his* world,
his private domain of mental illness and torture.
Guided by a living al-Bah'ram or by sensors and
scanners and ancient programming . . . King
Dragon is after me!

It has a kinship with other pterosaurs; it must
have some sort of link with them, a means of
controlling them!

Johara uttered a little cry and stared after him as
Allayth lurched to his feet. No longer aware of
her, he began excitedly thinking aloud.

"He *controls* his 'planned experiment in observed evolution!' A living God, 'paternal' and
seemingly benign . . . *for nine hundred years!*
Keeping 'his people' dependent. Keeping them
primitive! Allowing no swerving from the Way of
al-Islam in which he was always a fanatical
believer—and the language of its founders, too.
Allahuma! Sahr: assheduan!—O my God, blood-
revenge I swear!"

"My—my lion?"

"Checking an occasional set of *specimens by
having the Hajari fetch him random samples,
perhaps? By now he hs the memories of twelve
hundred years and more, stuffed to bursting with*

them—to cracking! An unstable fanatic and megalomaniac to begin with—and by now he is cracked wide open! Monster!"

"My lion—what is it? Please?" She was fearful; tearful.

He wheeled on her and she saw eyes that seemed to flame. A lion gone mad with knowledge and horror, revulsion; growing resolve.

"What is it? Daa al-Kabir! Great Evil, Joharah! Suppose he is King Dragon! Malik-rukh and al-Bah'ram: the same! Pure madness and evil. The Big Boss Bah'ram's messenger, sensor-spy, scanner, angel, devil . . . mobile eyes and even occasional voice, to keep his people in line on his planet—which is Hell!"

She flowed to her feet, staring stricken. Tears oozed. When he strode to her she shrank—but the hands on her upper arms were good, and his face lost its twist of rage: the rage of revelation. And at last Jimajin Allayth made a pure, non-reactive decision, to Do.

"Jo. We are leaving this cave. King Dragon is from . . . Iblees! From al-Barahut! From Hell-that-is-Earth, not from Allah at all! Allah has . . . tested Ajjer's people, and they have failed Him, by accepting King Dragon as God! I will try to explain as we go, but we are going. We are going to the den of a monster, however far it is. We may have to fight, but we'll get through. Scheherazade liberated only a city, a kingdom—we will liberate a planet, Johara! I know, I know," he said, with pain in his voice at her face, the incomprehension in her eyes. "I know, but I will try to explain as we go. We are going! Come on!"

The voice came from somewhere outside: "Johaaaarraaahh . . ."

19

At the sound of that awful call the blood drained from Johara's face as water rushes down a drain. The voice from outside was as one from the crypt, filtering up through crowding rocks. She clutched Allayth with both hands and her lithe body had gone rigid as dogma.

"JO-HAAARRRAAAHH . . ."

"*Raafar!*" she said, and Allayth, a few centimeters from her mouth barely heard her. He felt the fear-tightened clamp of her hands.

He had to twist from her grasp, and in that, one clutching hand scratched his arm. He plucked her dagger from her sheath but did not pick up the bow. Her hand clapped the empty sheath while he moved to the mouth of the cave, his other hand drawing the long-knife. His armpits prickled hot and his heartbeat was a tympanic stutter. His mouth had become a desert. On that ledge that now seemed to have narrowed to a mere ribbon of grey and ochre, he turned and looked up.

That beautiful-horrible-pathetic giant stood up there on the scarp's brink. He was hideous; he was frightening; he was magnificent. He stood tall against the sky and its empyrean light made him loom even larger and more dire. Bigger than Al-

layth in every way and more ugly than nightmares. Every superb muscle stood forth and rip-
pled in a gleaming elegance that proclaimed animal force.

Allayth stared up at him and Raafar looked
down on the smaller man.

As if in disdain, the Ajjeri threw down his spear
and shook a big round shield off an arm the size of
a leg. He still held what seemed a few thousand
kilos of ax. Allayth swallowed, He knew there was
sweat in the palms that clutched the hilts of a dead
man's weapons. Sheathing the dagger, he wiped
that hand on his furs, transferred the long-knife,
and wiped that hand.

"I am Raafar Saaurrslayerrr." The sound was
hideous, throaty and thick, bubbling from the
torn, scar-seamed face. "I want Johaaaraa."

Allayth swallowed again, although drought
had taken his mouth. "I am Jimajin Allay . . .
al-Layth," he amended, "of . . . Terra. She—"

Raafar bent tree-trunk legs, hefted the ax high in
a multiple scintillance of mica, and jumped down
the several meters to the ledge. Obviously there
was no time for the other man to meet that attack,
to do anything about it. He did; he did his best to
end it there and then, despite the suddenness of
the huge man's pounce. His empty fist slammed
into Raafar's midsection before his feet came
down on the shelf. Raafar grunted and doubled
over the fist and Allayth's arm hurt.

The giant twisted with an incredible feline
sinuousness that dropped him onto the ledge despite a gut-punch that should have sent him
backward into space and the long fall to the river
bank. His legs doubling like springs, he went low

while his ax smashed bits of stone from the hillside. It missed Allayth, who felt the impacts of
several shards of rock. At the same time, his knife
was slicing open the air above the grotesque head.
Raafar's right hand swept out then, at the end of
an arm nearly as big as the other man's thigh. This
time it was the Earthman whose stomach and leg
muscles tautened and bulged. Pain jagged
through stomach and thighs as he hurled himself
back out of reach with an effort possible only
because it was necessary. He tripped in that
backward lurch, and he fell.

Impact was hard but he had no time for pain just
now and so interferon intervened and pain was
damped. He rolled, felt a leg flail empty space
beyond the ledge, and twisted again. When he
rose into a crouch, so had Raafar. The giant
showed a discoloration on that washboard belly,
but no apparent pain or debilitation. He hefted his
ax. That mass of raggedy stone was enough to
crush the head of a bull, a tyrannosaur . . . or a
man named Allayth.

"Raafar Saurslayer! We have no quarrel. She
does not want to go with you, Raafar Saurslayer,
Leave it. Leave her."

"Ahhh." Glutinous, frightening, piteous
sound. "We do have quaaarrel. King Dragon told
me of you. The Lion, is it? From Shirrrzaaad,
perhaps. King Draaagon has told me of you. He
said you are all evil and sent from Hell, not our
own Ajjer. He says you must di-iee. It is the will of
al-Bah'raaam, be he blessed."

The sun was low behind Allayth, sending back
long streamers as if clinging to the sky. Behind the
homunculoid man the very sky seemed porten-
tously bloodshot.

"King . . . Dragon spoke to you? Recent? This day?"

"This daaay, demon from Earth-that-is-Iblees's domain. Yesss."

"Wait, Raafar Saurslayer. Where were you when Malik-rukh spoke to you? On the other side of a stream, perhaps?"

"Yesss. King Draagon guided me to youuu, demon. And to Johaaarah." The demon-face twisted out her name and Allayth glanced at the cave, just beside him. Here the ledge bent around the scarp. Two steps and Allayth would be around the bend of the hill; Raafar could not see into the cave.

"Huh. So you did not track us." Raafar seemed to diminish a bit, with that knowledge—but only a bit. "Best you go from here in peace, Saurslayer. Surely no man desires to be manslayer, not you and not I. Has King Dragon told you that I, Jimajin Dragonslayer, slew four dragons he sent to kill us? *Us*, both me and Johara? Has he told you that he attacked us, King Dragon himself, and that I drove him off? *I?*"

"Demons haave power over draaagons. Nothing has power over Raafar Saurrslayerrr."

Something did, Allayth thought. *Something made you the most pathetically hideous Adonis a twisted mind could ever conceive . . . golem!*

"Johara fears and abhors Raafar Saurslayer," he said quietly, very quietly. Two men, three meters apart on a shelf of rock less than a meter wide. "If you feel for her, love her, go from here. She is bow-armed; *armed with the bow*. Go in peace and honor, mighty Raafar, and let her be happy away from Kwait."

"I act for King Draaagon; for al-Bah'ram . . . for

Aallaah! Jo-haaara . . . does not matter. You I
must slay, demon!"

He charged along the ledge.

Allayth saw him squinting because the setting
sun was behind Allayth. Allayth swung back the
long knife for a chopping blow to match that of the
ax and he drew the dagger as the ax swung high.
Rather than await the charge and the ax's fall, he
lunged forward while the dagger came out and
from the hip he drove it straight at Raafar's belly.

At the last moment the giant realized the tactic
the stone age had never seen, the gutting street-
fighter's stroke of a dagger—and the sinister
power in the demon's left hand. The ax-stroke
shivered as he tried to readjust its timing and
swing while at the same time twisting himself
aside with the same magnificently muscled

strength that had saved him before. This demon
did not fight properly!

Already amove, Allayth had only to keep moving. With an extra step hastily added, he completed his thrust. The dagger went all the way into
Raafar's lower intestine and jolted Allayth's arm
past the shoulder.

The big man's hands, like his mouth snapped
wide in a reflex of shock and agony. Ice had slid
into his upper groin. The ax went flying from his
hand to fly crashing and banging down and
down, amid sparks and bits of stone from its blade
and from the hillside of rock.

Allayth's other hand came around then. The
long-knife chopped ten centimeters into Raafar's
muscular side. He groaned and muscles spasmed
while sphincters let go. As he staggered, twisting,
still moving with a dreadful superhuman volition, Allayth groaned at the pressure on his wrist.
The dagger remained imbedded, twisting in the
wound. And with both those wounds, the giant
was still reaching for him with hands that looked
big as baseball gloves.

Raafar's good eye caught a movement behind
Allayth, beside Allayth—

"Jo-ha—"

The bowstring twanged. The arrow rushed out
of the cave at a range of less than three meters and
struck into his left pectoral like the blow of a
hammer.

Only one of Raafar's hands slammed into Allayth's head. The other was wildly clutching air.
Allayth saw darkness spectacularly split open by
dancing lights. The force of that blow swept him
directly into the cave, like a small boy struck by an

angry parent. The dagger was forced out of the other man's bowels. Jim Allayth fell through the hole in the hillside without even seeing Raafar Saurslayer, legs limpening and arms windmilling, go silently backward off the ledge.

One man fell a couple of meters to lie unconscious; the other fell a tenth of a kilometer to splatter all over a jagged pile of rock.

20

The sun had set in blood and risen again in gold. On Earth, nearly three days had passed. That, however, was relevant to nothing. Nothing at all. All that was relevant now was a planet misnamed Heaven. It was where Jimajin Allayth was sure he would spend the rest of his life.

It was not a concept he had resigned himself to; that stage he had passed without pausing. First he had merely not accepted it. That was effected by his refusal to think about it, which was made easier by his being kept busy surviving. Thus he had not had to accept or to resign himself. Now he knew, just knew. He wasn't going back. He did not consider other possibilities and might-have-beens. Earth, with Cicada and *Cygnet* and Laxshimy and Flaerti and supposed aspirations to a societal goal called Scholardom, which he had thought was his goal—all were passed and part of the past.

Allayth thought of the past no more. Now was better. The future was better.

He had Johara, and that was better. Johara had him. He had awakened to find her holding him and weeping over him. He had fallen; Raafar had fallen; night had fallen.

He had himself, and this self was better. This self would not weep over him, not any more. This self was the future, and that was better than the past. This self—he—would make it so. The past was not better; it was a corpse, peopled with corpses. He, this self, would make the future better.

In that, Johara would be more than help. She was someone he could like as well as love, which came after the lust that often masqueraded as love. She was intelligent and she could talk and think and learn. Almost miraculously, considering what she had endured, Johara was strong and determined. She was decisive. No fearful little girl had made the enormous decision to leave Kwait rather than be mated with the horror of Raafar. She had considered, decided, and taken action. At the time, that was more than Jim Allayth would have done, and he knew it.

No squeaky "heroine" of too many romances had pounced to stab Abdulassan again and again because he was a menace to Jim Allayth.

No save-me save-me doll had sent an arrow into Raafar because he menaced her man and her future.

"Her lion" had acted, too, to become the protector she thought him. He had become her lion; lion to a lioness.

Still, he did not delude himself that he was an all-new man, that he would be instantly decisive and heroic all his life. Both implied and usually necessitated forging ahead, which was not the way of a highly intelligent and introspective man who so long sought; had so long been unsure. He was no damner of torpedoes and no espouser of the concept of When in doubt, Charge.

Johara would be more than companion and of

more than immense value. She was *necessary*. He
had learned that he was most definitely not a
loner. Not in living, not in acting, not in
decision-making.

He had told her how strong and important she
was and saw that she either did not understand or
did not accept. Her mental set came from her
culture. She was sure that she needed him and
leaned on him.She did, and by leaning, propped.
So did he. Yet he did not delude himself that they
would be one perfect inseparable team, a unit, as
was all of one couple he knew—had known. Only
one. No, he and Johara were surely slated for some
trouble. The gap, cultural and educational, lay
between them and was wider than had ever
existed between two humans. Each would surely
in future grow more impatient with the other, or
worse.

And just now he knew that it was rot to think
such thoughts.

Either of them might die at any time, suddenly
and horribly on this inimical planet. Both of them
might. Either or both could be maimed. This he
considered while they made their way down the
scarp and past the corpses of Raafar and the
twisted pterodactyl. Raafar had been a victim, a
figure of pathos in the same way as the Larry
Talbot figure in Earth's old werebeast legends.
Allayth was not happy that he had been forced to
slay—that they had, he and Johara. On a bad
planet operating at the whim of a man gone bad,
the death of a man who was not bad could not long
occupy anyone's thoughts. It was a minor incident, now. But for King Dragon, Raafar would not
have found them.

Just let us find King Dragon, Allayth thought.

Let me get near whatever creature wears the name
al-Bah'ram.

Allayth stopped then, thinking. He took
another step into another era, then; into the era
that was Ajjer. He and Johara used both knives
and after a while they needed bindings. She mentioned the twisty vine called splicer, whose
amber-green new shoots were cords that were excellent for binding. Unfortunately none grew on
that tall rocky hill or along the banks of the river.

They used strips of hide from poor Raafar's
blood-splashed garments.

Part of the hide and their staves, with a couple
of saplings and most of one wing of the dead
dragon, enabled them to cross the river. Two
water snakes accompanied them, but the olive-
hued creatures seemed only curious or perhaps
envious of the humans' vehicle. It was hardly the
most stable of craft, or the most pleasant of cross-
ings.

They reached the other shore well down-river
from the corpses of recent enemies, and rested
there. Talking, still getting acquainted across a
gap of centuries of technology, biology, psy-
chology—and sociology learned mostly from
mistakes. Neither of them admitted to a wary
watching of the sky or listening for the flap of
mighty wings. They entered the forest. Two
hyænodons snarled and slunk. A cat-sized lizard
raced up a tree and for no good reason Allayth
snatched at its electric blue tail. The creature went
off without it.

"Just what I always wanted," he muttered, feeling rather embarrassed.

Next he took time to uproot a twinerbitch, just

to feel that he had done something worthwhile.
And they went on, with him beginning to wonder
about other humans. How many Kwaits were
there? Suppose there was just one, and one
Hajarazad, and that was the sum total of humanity
on Ajjer? *And us. Will we found a community, a
village, a town, a city? Lord—what sort of father
am I likely to be?*

While he was relieving himself against a fat-
trunked ginkgoid a magenta-and-gold snake rose
to menace Johara, showing back-curving fangs,
and Allayth put an arrow through its head before
it struck. After he had chopped the body in two,
he retrieved the arrow. It was not a serpent of a
sort she had ever seen before. They had come far
and far. On Ajjer, no one traveled so far. Why
should anyone?

*I wonder if she and I have already started a
baby?*

He did not wonder about his ability, his reac-
tions, though it was new to him, this being a man
of swift action who reached for weapons and used
them with high competence, rather than going
into panic or missing because of what had once
been called buck fever. It was the way he was. He
supposed that he always had been. He just hadn't
known it; had not had opportunity to find out
what sort of man he was.

They ate fungi and superb tubers, nut-fruits
and, when they found it, the fleshy mushroom
called meatplant. He wished that he could find
something he could recognize as flint; that way he
could start a fire and they would be able to cook an
occasional meal. It occurred to him that she must
know how to make fire. He asked. Of course, she

said, and he nodded resignedly. Of course.

They cut spears that were really staves pointed on one end. She soon put hers to use, pinning a lizard half her size when it decided he looked tasty. It proved tasty, but later made them mildly sick. At least his system had adjusted to the planet enough so that he no longer had the runs all the time.

He slashed his forearm on a skeaner, a dagger-like plant that was indeed sharp along its rather hard, serrated leaf. She showed him that a tasty epiphytic aster in blue and cinnabar was good on wounds. To that she added the bark of a chittapel. The umbrella-like tree's sinewy inner bark was astringent, and the combination left him without pain or even itching. The wound healed rapidly and a day passed.

The night-light of the spirt was eerie. He captured two of the bulbs and handled them, wondering whether they might possibly be of any use in making fire. *I doubt it,* he thought examining one tautly swollen baseball-sized bulb and reflecting on the Terran firefly—and the spirt popped. The cloud of chlorous gas shot straight into his face and he passed out about the time he decided that he was dying.

He wasn't. When he awoke, the moon's position told him that he had been unconscious for about an hour. The headache lasted hours more.

That night he definitely saw and tracked the middle moon, while the nearest one—Shirzad—was racing around the other side of Ajjer. That was all. The planet had three satellites —not counting the Mausoleum. Having found and tracked two of them made Jim Allayth feel

very learned. The rest of the night he passed in snoozing and being a lover.

Two of the seven dinosaur eggs they found proved palatable indeed, each the equivalent of three or more normal eggs. He felt that Ajjer would be far better off for his smashing the rest of the amber ovals. That was five less uglies to have to worry about.

A short time later they met mama.

The blue-green anole was nine or so meters long, tail shimmy-slithering behind her like a pointed cable. Under her (his?) throat swelled a fat white-red puff pouch. The anole puffed it. It also chased them for about a half-hour and hung around under their arboreal refuge for a long, long time. They waited, with Allayth occupying himself in searching the sky for the moon—a moon— and sucking sweet sap from the long hairy creeper imaginatively called sweetclimber.

Far above them an archæopteryx drifted over with its lengthy spear-haft bill and tail fringed with feathers. Flapping southward, it paid them no attention at all. And of course something at last deflected the anole's short attention span. It departed, moving in squirts.

Johara and Jim were nearly down from their tree when they heard the crashing. It approached. A two-man tank at the very least was coming their way through the trees, and from the sound of it "through" was the proper word. They hastened back up into their haven and Johara discovered a way to cross into a far bigger tree. The maneuver did not involve swinging on a vine. Allayth learned one more good aspect of boots with flexible soles and no added heels.

The ridiculously long-necked saurian from the Jurassic era could easily have plucked them from their perch, had it desired. The diplodocus did not. It was interested only in leaves and loved pretty hanging blossoms so much it had developed the neck to get at them. The homely monster did half strip the tree they had quitted, including their former perch. Allayth and Johara waited. Only an idiot or a very, very hungry person would try tangling with that thing, vegetarian sauropod or not.

It was a long time moving on. Its tail followed, a gigantic worm of great weight. *Catch one and keep it for a pet*, Allayth mused inanely. *Feed it a few trees, twice a day. Name it Ouroboros.*

"Maybe we should just wait awhile," he said, when she began moving; their branch was after all wide as a double bed, if hardly so comfortable. "Maybe a kingsaur is tracking *that*."

"It is strange, my lion—a mighty hunter who is also wise."

"The other kind doesn't hunt for long," he said, and thought of Raafar and went silent and inward.

They heard nothing else, and descended.

All the rest of that day they saw no fauna bigger than an orange-and-bile-and-brown lizard with a sail-like frill as wide as the length of Allayth's bow. They made a lot of noise, vocally and by banging their staffs on the bole of a dead but standing tree. The tree held and so did the staffs. The big frilled lizard departed, either frightened or esthetically revolted.

Toward sunset they thought they saw King Dragon, but thought that he did not see them. Allayth recounted his arrows. That did not take long. Nor did it require the use of ten fingers.

The moons raced around the planet which meandered around the sun and rain came and fungi shot up and up and a man and a woman loved in the dark, and slept, and talked and talked. The sun returned, and another rain, in which they bathed naked. The green nut-fruits that had hung nearby were ripe and ready for breakfast.

That day they tried to do something about more arrows, without much result. Johara had never made one either.

Ferny fronds parted and a puma-sized spotted cat stared at Allayth with eyes like fine topaz. He slipped the string on his bow and reached for an arrow—slowly, so as not to alarm the predator. Her hand touched his wrist, gently pressing.

"Spotcat is not hungry and is a coward too, and we are not in need of clothing."

"A wild feline? A *coward*?"

Yes, for at sound of his querulous voice the source of Ajjeran clothing hastily backed and vanished.

Another biological construction through use of recombinant DNA, he mused as they moved on. *A cowardly leopard, with the trait made hereditary! Did al-Bah'ram have that much respect for leopards, or hatred, or . . . could the old monster possibly have a sense of humor?*

Hours and kilometers later she spent a long hour showing him how a snakerloo seemed to follow her. The vine, whose blooms were the color of fresh cinnamon, did, though hardly as rapidly or rapaciously as a twinerbitch. Watching it weave, snakelike, until it found her location was eerie. He wondered whether the creeper could have any sentience, and decided certainly not. It must follow heat, when it had the opportunity. He assumed. Probably.

How many subjects for Original Contributions there were on Johara al-Ajr!

At the edge of a swamp they decided to skirt, she spotted a stand of spiculdag. Solemn spears standing sentry over the torpid water. The stem of the pre-cattail was hairy and just under two meters long, running up and up into an arrowhead cap. The thing was *hard.* They cut several, wincing at the hair-touches that made them want to scratch arms and the backs of hands. With care so that it did not fall on their legs, they scraped off the hair.

The result was a whippy, thumb-thick mace of glaucous white. They took several. In a few days, Johara pointed out, the spiculdags would make decent light spears.

As they moved on, she warned him that they must be careful when the thing began to approach the fully dry state. The hard spicule cracked open to emit its aerogenic seeds, and became immediately rot-soft.

The seeds were not poisonous, at least.

Not everything on Ajjer is inimical by any means, he reminded himself as they made their way around the misty swamp. It took on a particularly unpleasant green glow as the sun sank lower and lower. Shirzad came and went, the sun died, and they had not quite reached the far end of the pear-shaped swamp. Here, though, was a little flood-pool or detached estuary, which they knew the darkrain would freshen nicely. They stopped, collected a fungoid and floral dinner, and waited for darkrain. Johara sat domestically demonstrating how mothers plaited loincloths for their children, using absorbent "leaves" of a quillwort called sloper.

"Of course we women wear them a few days each month, too," she said easily, her eyes on her work. Vision was nearly gone.

He thought immediately of a discussion with a woman named Cicada, somewhen on the order of ten or eighty years ago. That saddened him and reminded him of time, which reminded him of a man-into-god called al-Bah'ram. Could he possibly still be alive?

"Then one ties a nice knot on the hip. Left for girls, right hip for boys. The mother's knot. Do you think we will have boys and girls both?"

If he is still alive, or again-and-again alive through cloning and some RNA fanciwork plus a bit of simple recom-deenay adjusting, he must be

. . . *weary. Sad. And certainly half mad. More likely—*

"Here, I shall model it for you. Infant Joharah, see? My lion?"

—less than half sane! A bloody lunatic up there ahead somewhere—westward, ever westward—an amplified man (of diminished brain/sanity!) with his bio-implants. An exoskeleton, maybe, with built-in motors and sensory feedback from ole King Dragon? The way he controls his filthy K—

"My lion? Are you paying no attention at all? Are you so accustomed to the sight of me already? I begin to feel ashamed just stand—*My Lion!*"

His head came up at that shriek. In horror he saw the great veined, ragged sail rising behind her, heard the patter of water running from the dark figure of horror slowly rising from the water in which it had taken refuge, wounded—or lain in wait for this ambush. Now he rose behind the almost naked woman—Jimajin Allayth's woman. K—

"*—ing Dragon!*"

The arrow was gone from between the eyes, which Allayth was seeing for the first time at night. They were noctiluminescent—or more likely not biological eyes at all, but electroscanners. And behind them relays, instant transmittal telemetry. Transmitting in garbles, because of the arrow? Was the thing watertight? Had it fallen into the pool or was it lying in wait here for them?

The night-black wing folded around the nearly nude woman, and the horrid yellow eye of that ominous prodigy glowed inimically, glittered
. . .

A man in a leopard skin breechclout charged silently in a blind mix of fear and rage and hatred no less mindless and superhuman than those Nordic ancients called *baresarks*, berserkers, and he too was bare of sark or shirt, a raging running savage clad only in his tail-trailing breechclout of spotted hide. A long blade glittered in his hand.

Claws tangled in the onyx cobwebbery of Johara's hair and she screamed, twisting, lashing backward with elbows and fists while Allayth's fur boots slopped through shoreline muck and splashed into the pool. Water flew noisily high and King Dragon rose higher and higher and from the throat of the charging man of technocratic, spacefaring civilization bellowed forth an elemental cry; the purely savage roar of a man whose mate was endangered.

He bounded up out of the water in a mad leap that carried him past Johara and onto the Cretaceous nightmare spawned from madness and high technology.

King Dragon fell back, emitting a strangely hollow cry. The clawed wing jerked spasmodically up and back. Strands of hair came loose in those almost-fingers while Johara flew three meters to splash windmilling into the murky waters of the swamp. Allayth had a flash of Cicada flying through the air—

The long-knife plunged into King Dragon's neck and through it and out and into it again while the toothy gargoyle beak gaped and clacked and clawed almost-hands tore at the maniacal human atop him.

The creature flopped, twisted, somehow got it-

self out of the water. Somehow it hurled Allayth from it, somehow gained its feet. It ran, lizard-like but lurching, rocking big wings back and forth, leaking blood (yes, blood), using wings and tail to steady itself, trying to flap.

That it was not going to get itself into the air was obvious. So was the fact that a wounded Malik-rukh was fleeing, unable to cope, panicking. (An old old man desperately manipulating his controls, too many memories, so long attuned to the outsize modified pterosaur that he was a part of the beast he had designed too many memories ago, created to be a part of him. Too many memories—rage—how did this puny silly man dare get away try to stop him from getting away and away up high in the too many memories far too wet and hurt to get off the rage off the ground

run run ground is he coming coming coming to
kill kill rage kill them all not worthy anyhow
horrid mortal humans kill going to have to [get
away] kill them all cleanse the planet the red
button red button button red pain and dimming
vision red button [is this panic?] rage . . .

Wallowing and floundering, Allayth was sin-
gle-minded or un-minded. His blade dripped.
King Dragon was wounded and Johara had been
thrown the same way Cicada had been thrown
and this time the monster would not escape if Jim
Allayth had to run all night.

Water sloshed and squished in his boots as he
hurled himself floundering after the fleeing
monster.

"Wait for me, King Demon!" he bawled.

King Dragon heard and relayed what he heard
blundering fleeing floundering, a landbound flying biomachine to which its glorious wings were
now only a liability.

"Wait for me, King Demon, al-Bah'ram! Wait,
you sick old monster! Will you feel it when I catch
your construct and carve it up? Can you still believe you are God when I come from His heavens
and chase your machine-thing of evil? Allah
wants His people to develop, al-Bah'ram, King
Monster, not be held back by a sick old man and
his flying *demon!*"

(He knows he knows red red pain button too
many memories but he will never catch never
have all this glorious home of God's Own Representative God god I am God could he be right
right too many mem the red button brings release
pain chasing chased red sets off every charge
every last charge in the no no must continue to do

God's wor—could he be right right red rage right red red pain button rage)

"I am Allaahhh!" King Dragon bellowed or tried to, and blood burbled from its pierced neck while the pursuing man goosefleshed—and followed. Blindly, irrationally. *Johara!* Cerebration was fled and pointed, edged weapons were in hand. Now his squishing sloshing squelching furboots were out of the water and on land *Johara!* while the ungainly creature fled and fled into the night. It tried to dodge rearing trees and fungi and ran into them instead, rebounding, ran into them and over them, between them tearing wings, great wings flapping and flopping as it tried and tried to gain the air . . .

—and could not.

Allayth ran, long-knife and dagger waving from white-knuckled fists. The frenetic moon appeared and tried to race the ungainly grounded pterosaur and the running man. Three shapes in night of onyx and sky of indigo against which trees rose like columns of basalt.

(My baby my life my Self! Should have had another ready as one more clone still floats ready with too many memories but how could I too many memories could I? I am part of him! My eyes my Eyes my very Eyes they—he are is part of me part of each other could he be right is this insanity part of too many memornever let that evil creature from Earth home of Eblees have all this my home all implanted and laced with charges red button red pain bringing peace surcease in the red b only for Allah, only for Thee, my God never for humans silly horrid unworthy mortals run seeking peace the peace that lies in the red button no no why won't it leave me alone?—glowing so redly why won't he leave me alone tugging at my eyes red my eyes? Peace O Allah, all I seek is peace in thy Name but but button but)

Allayth overtook the long serpentine tail and hacked it. He bounded on, overhauled the fleeing monster. He hacked the lower backbone and stabbed a wing (pain!—pain!—red pain red red tugging at my eyes my Eyes my Eyes he is killing my Eyes) and hacked a wing backswinging to hack the backbone and into the neck, hacking and hacking while the head twisted and wings flapped and flopped. Blood spattered and bits of metal implant flew in air glittering beneath the rushing moon and he hacked, hacked. Clawed "fingers" flew and pain *was* imparted to the ancient man; surely it was only in his mind that he *was* linked) while King Dragon writhed, flopped (to the Eyes, his Eyes and Messenger; had been for years, decades, centuries of too many memories. Pain pain hurt it hurt the Eyes were being killed, killed, his mighty spy-roc killed and it hurt despite logic for it was only a modified Thing, a semi-construct but O the pain oh) and blood bubbled and Allayth hacked until King Dragon lay dead in the moonlight, dead in pieces, and somewhere a strangely-gloved, arthritic hand jerked and rushed in blind un-sane panic to depress a dull, unlit red button.

Loinclothed, a weapon dripping in each hand, Jimajin al-Layth returned to the rain-pool. He found his woman there, pale and waiting, bow in hand and eyes large and bright with concern.

"I am all right," he told her.

"I am all right," she said.

Red-smeared weapons of iron, dulled against hide and bone and plastic and steel, dropped from his hands and he embraced her, bare skin to bare wet skin. Lord Jimajin the Lion embraced his woman and claimed her lips and did not lift his head until the night sky was turned into day, brightness at midnight, by the multiple explosions resulting from a thousand-year-old brain's guiding an arthritic finger to depress a button red as blood.

Maybe, Jim Allayth thought next day, *by the time we get her back to Kwait I'll have figured a way to organize her people, get them to help me find the jumpship. There's bound to be all sorts of usable materiel there. Maybe by then too we will have decided, together, on a way to let them know there is no more King Dragon . . . and no more living god on Ajjer.*

POUL ANDERSON

FRITZ LEIBER

FAFHRD AND THE GRAY MOUSER SAGA

79175	SWORDS AND DEVILTRY	$1.95
79155	SWORDS AGAINST DEATH	$1.95
79184	SWORDS IN THE MIST	$1.95
79164	SWORDS AGAINST WIZARDRY	$1.95
79223	THE SWORDS OF LANKHMAR	$1.95
79168	SWORDS AND ICE MAGIC	$1.95

H. Beam Piper

☐ 24890 **Four Day Planet/Lone Star Planet** $2.25

☐ 26192 **Fuzzy Sapiens** 1.95

☐ 48492 **Little Fuzzy** 1.95

☐ 49052 **Lord Kalvan Of Otherwhen** 1.95

☐ 77781 **Space Viking** 1.95

Available wherever paperbacks are sold or use this coupon.

- -